notes from the
# TEENAGE
# UNDERGROUND

# notes from the
# TEENAGE
# UNDERGROUND

*a novel*

## Simmone Howell

BLOOMSBURY

Published by Bloomsbury U.S.A. Children's Books
175 Fifth Avenue, New York, NY 10010
Distributed to the trade by Holtzbrinck Publishers

Library of Congress Cataloging-in-Publication Data
Howell, Simmone.
Notes from the teenage underground / by Simmone Howell.—1st U.S. ed.
p.    cm.
Summary: Seventeen-year-old film buff Gem sets out to make an underground movie with her friends Lo and Mira, but discovers much about her own life in the process.
ISBN-13: 978-1-58234-835-3 • ISBN-10: 1-58234-835-9
[1. Motion pictures—Fiction. 2. Friendship—Fiction. 3. Coming of age—Fiction.]
I. Title.
PZ7.H8383No2007                [Fic]—dc22                2006018512

First U.S. Edition 2007
Typeset by Westchester Book Composition
Printed in the U.S.A. by Quebecor World Fairfield
10  9  8  7  6  5  4  3  2  1

All papers used by Bloomsbury U.S.A. are natural, recyclable products made from wood grown in well-managed forests. The manufacturing processes conform to the environmental regulations of the country of origin.

*For Mark and Willeford*

*Long live the underground!*
*The devil take the underground!*
—Dostoevsky

notes from the
# TEENAGE
# UNDERGROUND

# GOING UNDERGROUND

# *Blank Canvas*

Things I love about the National Gallery:

- How on the outside it looks like a big public toilet block but inside it's full of treasure
- How running my hand along the water wall at the entrance makes me feel five years old and daring
- How gallery goers are either looking to get lost or pretending that they're not
- How in the Great Hall, when the sun shoots through the stained-glass ceiling, lost or not, people's faces take on rainbows

· · ·

On the day of the gallery excursion, me, Lo, and Mira had met early at HQ, the disused junior school toilet block. Escape from school and our backwater suburb, no matter how brief, required prep work. We passed around our artillery: cigarettes, mascara, and hot mocha lip tint, all the while teeming with the prospect of the city. We were late for the bus, but that was to be expected. As we walked up, with our arms linked and attitudes on full beam, I thought, "Moments like these are the best." Me, Lo, and Mira were like the good things that came in threes: wishes, kings, backup singers. But we could be bad too. We climbed aboard the bus. Bliss Dartford—miss priss popularity—sang out, "Here come the frrrreaks!" and the sucker peers stirred and snickered but this just confirmed what we already knew: we were cool, unique, original. Everybody else was bar code.

· · ·

At the gallery, we checked our bags and dragged along with the group, past Greek urns, Dutch masters, and Royal turds, into the moderns. Our gender-trauma art teacher Barry "Boobs" Polson had us all camp before a painting with our notebooks open.

"Think about what you see," he instructed. "Write it down."

The painting was completely and utterly black. It made me think of nighttime. I wondered if there was anything underneath its shiny surface. Things impressionable young girls shouldn't be looking at. I wrote in my notebook: *Surface and Underneath.*

I felt my face. Beneath the frizz and lippy I looked like a normal seventeen-year-old. Brown eyes, brown hair, combination skin. I was meant for bigger things. My mother, Bev, named me after her favourite feminist, Germaine Greer. My namesake was brave and audacious, a sexual libertine, *and* an authority on Shakespeare. Um . . . much to live up to? If she was an icon, I was a clod. I could be boastful and call myself an authority on film, but there was no getting around my virginity. Bev insists that all smart girls have an inner Greer. I pictured mine asleep under a rock or a kidney stone. She wasn't likely to crawl out anytime soon.

I wrote in my notebook: *Everything and Nothing.*

I looked up. A couple of nerdburgers had their heads down, scribbling away but the rest of the class were passing notes or looking around the room, distracted. Boobs saw none of this. He was staring into the black, transfixed. He didn't even notice when Lo stuck me in the ribs and whispered, "Let's go."

. . .

Minutes later, the three of us were sitting on the grass in the sculpture garden, half hidden by a Henry Moore, sharing cigarettes and cashews and dreaming aloud.

Mira took her shoes and socks off. She stretched her legs out and inspected them. There was a line on her upper thigh where she'd stopped shaving. "God," she said. "Check me out."

"You're European," I stated. "If we lived there, we could spend our summer sleeping on the Riviera beaches. You wouldn't even have to shave."

Lo said, "Get thee to a depilatory."

"We could burn up Florence with scooter boys," I continued. "After dark we could dance barefoot in nightclubs, wearing only sheer green shifts with gold jewellery."

"Ha!" Mira smiled.

But Lo had had enough of my reverie. She nabbed my cigarette and took a drag. "I'm bored."

"You're always bored," I said.

Lo played the sullen blonde, from her purple toenails to her cig-smoky halo. Lo has talents. She is quick and merciless and she has perfected the art of looking put-upon. This makes people take her seriously.

She settled back on her elbows. "Summer lies before us like a . . ." She snapped her fingers, searching.

"Blank canvas?" I supplied.

"Exactly. We need a project."

"Well, it's that time of year," I said. "Are we still going to have a theme?"

"Of course!" Lo snapped. "And goals and guides. But whatever the theme is, it has to be *significant*."

"Significant how?" Mira asked.

Mira's secretary specs make her look bookish but her mouth always gives her away. Her lips have a life of their own. They remind me of that famous painting—Man Ray's kiss floating in the clouds. They can be floppy, foolish, soft, or sultry; it depends on what she's saying. Now she was pouting: "I thought this summer was going to be about boys."

"Boys, sure." Lo didn't blink. "Boho boys. Dangerous boys. Boys without bar codes."

"Do they exist?" I asked.

Ninety percent of the male population are bar code boys, mass-market items, straight off the production line. Bar code boys are irrefutably blah. Definitely *not* wish-list candidates. The only thing they're good for is practice.

"Forget about the boys!" Lo snapped again. "Think about the theme. God. How did you two ever manage without me?"

Mira and I shared a quick grin. We shrugged, and said in unison, "We didn't."

# *History*

Flashback to year seven.

Most of the class had bonded at the local primary school. Not me. Not Mira. When it came to "cliquing" up, we were like the bad chocolates left in the box. Marzipan and Turkish delight. Only for the weak-willed and desperate. I can blame Bev for my handmade clothes and hippie taint, but where do you cut the cord? I was arty and shy. I felt like I'd been given a different textbook to everyone else, one that didn't even have diagrams. Meanwhile, Mira was gauche-girl. Too enthusiastic by half. Always walking in on the end of jokes and laughing like she got them. The jokes were usually about her. She was fatter back then and had adenoidal issues. She sounded like a dirty phone call.

Mira and I drifted together, united in our quest for acceptance. We knew that cracking Bliss Dartford was the key. Every school has a Bliss—rich bitch, even tan, perfect orthodontics. Mira and I tried hard to impress her, but it wasn't happening. Then, in year eight, Mira's dad got promoted to corporate bigwig, and a whole new social strata opened up for her. I was left surfing the scummy edges.

How shallow is high school? Mira dropped a few pounds, started wearing labels, and her stock skyrocketed. When her mother started playing tennis with Bliss's mother, I knew it wouldn't be long before Bliss came around. I also knew that their "besties" status was temporary. Boys took care of that. Bliss may have been prettier, but Mira gave up the goods without even blinking. All year nine I watched them tango. Things were about to change. I could feel it.

Lo transferred three weeks into first term of year ten. She was so slight and quiet we hardly noticed her at first. Or maybe our receptors were blocked. By May she was coming in loud and clear. Was it the essay she read comparing Kurt Cobain's suicide note with Hamlet's third soliloquy? Or was it her negative care factor? Lo wore ankle socks to everyone else's knee socks, she didn't bother to comb her hair, she had cigarettes in her blazer pocket, and seemed to pick and choose her hours. Once, on the bus, I saw her skirt ride up. She had little nicks on her upper thigh. I remember pointing them out to Mira. She shrugged. "Freaks and geeks," but to me they hinted at a great dark past and made Lo fascinating. It took six months for Lo to rumble Bliss Dartford, rescue me, and recruit Mira. But this saving business works both ways. Lo said the cuts were just her way of marking time, keeping herself company. She doesn't do it anymore, not now that she has us.

.  .  .

Lo reminds me of this sweet-silly film *I Love You, Alice B. Toklas!* Peter Sellers plays a lawyer who drops out during the Summer of Love. Everything is groovy until all the pot and posturing start to go to his head. "I'm so hip it *hurts*," he whines to Leigh Taylor-Young, his chesty squeeze. She tells him, "It's very unhip to say that you are hip." Anyway, Lo's like that. She doesn't have to talk about being cool—she just is.

# *Themes, Goals, Guides*

Our summer project started as a joke. Every year for English Studies, our class is assigned a theme to go with our set texts. (This year it's "The Politics of Power" alongside *The Prince* by Machiavelli.) This time last year Lo decided the three of us should have a covert theme all our own. Only it would be more like an anti-theme, something edgy to enhance our outsider status, something that no school board would ever allow. She nominated "All Things Occult" and we spent the summer—dubbed Satan Summer—exploring the dark side.

It was only natural that Lo should rebel against her parents—they're born-again, seriously gothic. Mira and I, sick of same-old–same-old summers, were more than willing to be swept up in Lo's game. We each had a goal: Lo's was to get out of Christian camp; Mira's was to corrupt some brother school boys, and mine was to short-circuit my mother's foray into the world of Internet dating. Our "guides" were the famous or infamous historical figures whose lives we gleaned for inspiration. Our main man was Aleister Crowley—legendary magician and deviant. His credo, "Do what thou wilt is the whole of the law" (olde worlde speak for "Do whatever and don't apologise") became our license to fun. Our activities included but were not limited to

- hanging out at Inez Wisdom's Esoteric Emporium, plundering her Wicca library;
- watching endless horror movies;
- chanting incantations;
- propagating herbs, and
- etching pentagrams into public property.

Those were heady times. But I didn't doubt Lo could come up with something to match them.

# One word, three syllables

Lo snapped off a blade of grass and wound it around her fingertip, tighter and tighter until her skin went white.

"We should stage a protest or start a riot." Her voice was slow and thick, like she'd just come back from the dentist.

"But don't we need a cause?" I wondered aloud.

"I already gave you one." Lo sighed and shifted. "Boredom?" She looked around us, pointing at statues and picking off random gallery goers with her fingers. "Boring. Boring. Boring. Boring."

"Okay, we get it," I said.

We were quiet awhile. And then I thought of something interesting.

"Back in the eighties art terrorists stole a Picasso. They said they were going to burn it unless the arts minister coughed up more funding for young artists. They sent a burnt match with the ransom note and then noth-ing for ten days."

Lo sat up, just slightly. "So what happened?"

"There was a tip-off. They found the painting in a locker at Spencer Street station—deframed, rolled up, but otherwise unharmed. We went past it earlier. It's the one called *Weeping Woman*."

"Did they ever find out who did it?" Lo asked.

I shook my head.

Lo's eyes were lake-still and serious. "God, wouldn't you just want to tell someone?" She meditated on that thought for a while and then asked, "Do art terrorists still exist? Or is it just the other, everyday suicide kind?"

"I don't know," I said. "I could always ask Bev."

My mother is an art teacher. She's how I knew the story in the first place. She's how I know most things, when it comes right down to it.

Lo lit up a cigarette, suddenly animated. "I love it! That's what we should do this summer."

"Steal a Picasso?"

"No!" She was up and pacing, waving her hands about. "We should do cool, arty shit."

I nudged Mira. "Look out . . ."

Mira smiled, eyebrows on high.

Lo had gone into her fevered priestess pose—body still, eyes closed, face vibrating. She opened her eyes a few seconds later.

"I have the theme," she announced. She took a deep breath. "One word, three syllables: *Underground!*"

I bunched my brow while Lo scattered words like lawn seed.

She said, "We should be extreme, avant-garde, debauched, antiestablishment, revolutionary!"

"Doesn't sound very tan-fastic," Mira muttered.

"So go hang with Bliss," Lo returned. "I'm sure she'd welcome you back with open arms. You can have pool parties all summer long. Ad hoc day spas. Adventures in retail."

Anyone else would have taken this as an insult, but Mira just made a gagging noise. "Please! Don't make me go back there."

I watched my friends deflecting off each other, the sun tracking the silver in the stonework. I felt inspired, surrounded by art and possibility. When Lo got into something, she really got into it. Her enthusiasm was contagious, but also a little unsettling. She would whisk me and Mira into her whirling dervish, and once we were in there anything could happen. Lo was dancing with our theme now, teasing the word with her tongue, drawing it in, drawing it out. "Underground . . . Underground . . ."

She sat back down between us and drummed her knees and smiled, happy and childlike. "We'll call it Ug for short."

Mira leaned forward. "Ug-ug," she mugged. Then she checked herself, cleared her throat, and started spit-polishing her specs. This could only mean one thing. Boys were approaching. Ug would have to wait.

# Incoming!

Boy number 1 had a rocker quiff and a granddad suit-jacket festooned with punk badges. Lo said under her breath, "Bar code cool," which meant cool in quotemarks, but I was prepared to give him the benefit of the doubt. Boy number 2 was short and spotty, clearly the brains of the operation. He reached into his battered briefcase, brought out a postcard, and offered it to us. Lo deliberately looked at the sky; Mira blinked, blind without her glasses; so even though I was the farthest away *and* the least brave it was up to me to move our interaction along. I put out my hand and took the card. The graphic was from a children's annual—ruddy-cheeked boys and girls at play, only when I looked closely I saw that their eyes and mouths had been blacked out. The effect was jarring and creepy. I moved on to the typewritten text.

"What does it say?" Mira asked, in between making moues at Quiff.

"*A Clockwork Orange,*" I read.

Spots stepped up. "It's a new club. Friday nights at the back of the Bug Bar. It's on Elizabeth Street. Near the old post office."

He scanned our faces for recognition and came up short.

"We're from out of town," Lo said.

"But not out of the state." My contribution was innocuous, delivered in an uneven tone. I cringed inside, *here we go . . .*

Conversing with boys was such a trauma. Whenever the three of us happened upon male potential, I always wound up hovering at the sidelines, smiling stupidly, waiting for an in. When I did speak, it was never worth the effort. Maybe it was because I'd grown up without a male presence. Or maybe it was like Bev said—I was a late bloomer. No matter how you looked at it, when it came to the opposite sex I was officially at sea. Not so Lo and Mira—they were old salty dogs! They had different approaches: Mira was a maniac for boys—she billed and cooed and had a 100 percent success rate. Lo was Miss Ambivalence. In Satan Summer, Mira and I tried to give her grief because Jerome Packington was in hot pursuit. J-Roam, as he tags himself, is a great-looking moron. Bar Code Bad Boy. Mira and I were like, what a dream to have this hotness at your disposal. Lo said he only liked her because she black-magicked him, but that was nearly a year ago, and he still gives her longing looks across the food court.

I passed Lo the postcard. Her eyebrows lifted a little at the defaced kiddies, then she sighed and used the card to fan her face. Quiff was standing with his hands in his jacket pocket, his hip jutting out.

"It's a cool gig," he drawled.

Lo said, "How would *you* know?"

He started to answer, then stopped, disarmed. Lo thought flirting was for the birds. I had to hand it to her—she really knew how to knock them off their perches.

Spots asked Mira for a cigarette. She complied with an incandescent smile. Then, like a ritual, we all took one. Lo held her lighter out and let the boys hover in front of her. This was bad. They were blocking my sun. I was literally cast into shadows.

My face was starting to hurt. I forced myself to speak. "So what is it—everyone in boiler suits listening to Beethoven?"

At first, no one responded.

"*A Clockwork Orange,*" I explained. "The movie? The main character listens to Beethoven and . . ." My voice faded into the yawning pit of incomprehension. One of the side effects of my film-buffery was that I overestimated everyone else's interest. But I was making steps to improve this. Once upon a time I would have gone on an extended jag about how the director Stanley Kubrick pulled the ultraviolent film out of circulation because of death threats and copycat crimes. Lo would have liked this story, but Quiff was studying his filter tip and Spots just looked confused.

Mira exhaled a cough that sounded suspiciously like a laugh. Lo put her arm around my shoulder and said, "Gem's our film girl." She'd done this to make me feel better, but it had the opposite effect. I felt like a mascot. I shrank back. For the next few minutes there was small talk, banter, but it had nothing to do with me. There was a tightness growing in my stomach. I was thinking that Mira being all obvious and Lo being all anti made me about as memorable as grey matter. Finally, the boys showed signs of moving on.

Spots said, "So, maybe we'll see you there?"

Mira uncrossed and recrossed her legs. "Maybe . . ."

Quiff nodded. Spots made a fist: "Rock!" And off they loped, destroying all cool with a backward glance.

Lo had been waiting for that. She had her lighter ready, and as they looked back she flicked it, setting the post-card alight.

Mira snatched the burning card and clapped it between her hands. Lo stared at her. "You're unbelievable!"

"We might need it," Mira said. She looked down, smiled, and flicked the ash with her fingernails. "They were cute."

Lo snorted. "They were *schoolboys*!" She nudged me, trying to coax a smile. "Look what they did to Gem! She's gone all null."

That was me, null and void. I ground my cigarette into the grass. My head was aching. The sun seemed too bright. I stood up, mumbled something about needing water, and walked back into the gallery through the sliding glass doors.

# Infinite Loop of Kisses

En route to the toilet, by way of twentieth-century American art, I was drawn to lights flashing from a small alcove. I wandered in and sat on a low black couch opposite four television screens. The placard read *Andy Warhol, Kiss, 1963*. Four films were showing—all of couples kissing. They were close-ups in black and white; the only differences were in the details. Some couples were man-woman; some were man-man; and some you couldn't tell. The action was slowed down, like a dream—a disconcerting, scratchy, stop-start dream, but nothing like any dreams I knew.

In my dreams I was a kissing connoisseur. I had a bar code boy to practice on. His lips were hard, but soft, and his tongue was like a butterfly trapped in my mouth. Sometimes his hands would travel south; at that point my body double—the one who had no problem with nudity

and knew exactly what went where and for how long—
would take over.

I was glad the lights were low, that I was alone. I felt a
little uncomfortable watching. There was too much reality on-screen. In a thousand and one Hollywood movies
I'd never seen kisses like these. They were lips lunging,
eyes shifting, foreheads buckling, noses knocking, and
tongues flexing. They looked like hard work.

The films stopped and started up again. I stayed put.
Even though I knew what was coming I couldn't look
away. And something else—I was starting to get emotional. My throat was thickening up. There was no reason
for this. The films themselves were devoid of sentiment.
There was no sweeping score. No tragedy. But there was
also no mistaking that feeling—sadness—as distinct and
silly as the girl's bouffant on screen number 2.

Bev says that art only becomes Art when it makes you
think. As I studied the labouring lips, I was thinking this:
it would be something to have a boy to kiss. And the rest.

I was a girl on the back foot. Year eleven was *the* year
to lose your virginity, and now it was almost over. Everyone was into it. Churchy girls, maths-heads, sportos; it
was like every Monday someone else would walk in with
a new slouch. I didn't care about *them*, but Lo and Mira
were among the initiated, and it was hard not to feel left
out. Mira couldn't see where the problem was. "Just do
it!" she'd cry. "Pick a boy, get drunk, angle yourself appropriately." Lo was frustratingly quiet on the subject.
Thus the conundrum: I wanted to be different—but not

*that* different. I wanted to be casual, but I just couldn't
fake it.

About every other year the Midday Movie Show
screens *Between the Darkness and the Dawn*. It's about a
teenage girl who falls into a coma and awakens as a thirty-
seven-year-old virgin. She had a rare form of encephalitis.
I had no excuse.

Lo and Mira found me. They came in laughing, stinking
of smoke and secrets. The room felt suddenly crowded.
Mira bobbed and weaved in front of the screens. Lo slid up
the seat next to me. "How long have you been in here?"

"I don't know." This was true—it could have been five
minutes or fifty. The kissing continued in an infinite
loop.

"Are you getting lessons?" Mira teased. She went right
up close to kiss the screen. Lo laughed with her. On
screen number 3, a man's tongue poked into a waiting
mouth.

"Gross." Mira twitched.

"Come on." Lo shook my arm. "Boobs will be beside
himself."

# Carnal Knowledge

"So," Lo said in her "officious" voice, "re: Underground, aka Ug. We should hit the State Library on Saturday. We need goals and guides."

We were at the back of the school bus. The air around us was warm and smelled like old fruit and sports socks.

"Aren't you forgetting about exams?" I asked.

"Pass," Mira joked.

"You won't," I warned her.

"I don't care," Mira insisted. She sucked on her bottom lip.

"We've still got study week." Lo folded her arms across her chest. "Anyway, Ug will be educational."

"I can go Saturday morning, but I have to be back earlyish. I've got a date with Bev." I winced, but it was more for effect than anything else.

"Dinner and a movie," Mira baited me. "You're too weird."

"It's called bonding," I said.

"It's called creepy."

I raised an eyebrow at her and settled back in my seat. I almost said, "Jealous much?" but the truth was we all had a bit of green for each other. Pointing out Mira's would only give her cause to harp on mine.

Bev and I watch movies together. We always have. Sometimes we do it with ceremony—say there are a couple of hours reserved of a Saturday evening for Bev's and my "we" time. We make dinner and watch a movie, and then we pick through the holes in its plot. Sometimes we just watch whatever's on the boob. The point is we do it together. I understood Mira's "creepy" call. With her mother, it would be. There are only so many repressed housewives/Tuscan farmhouses/quirky villagers you can watch before rigor mortis of the mind sets in. But Bev has taste, and I have access to weird and wonderful films. Together we are a formidable team.

"Friday then," Lo decided. "After school. Can you work with that, Gem-Gem?" She slapped the seat, trying to rev me up, and I stamped my feet on the linoleum floor. Mira actually started chanting softly, "Ug-ug-ug-ug," until Lo gave her a look like, "Get excited, but not *too* excited."

It took forever to get back to school. There was a lane closed on the freeway. The bus moved through the traffic like a slug, and all the while images from the Warhol film kept returning to me. The afternoon sun had turned the windows to mirrors. My reflection was jowly, sulky. I reminded myself of a cod. I felt like crying.

"Here's a thought," I said. "Imagine that the social order is reversed. Beautiful boys go out with ugly girls and vice versa."

Mira cried, "You're not ugly!"

"You're unconventional," Lo said.

"I wasn't talking about me!" I snapped. But my voice was stitched with hurt. I felt them exchange a look. The sunlight shifted, dazzling us momentarily.

"Can my goal be to get a boyfriend?" I asked.

Lo said, "It would be more Ug if you had a series of lovers."

"I'll probably never have sex." I sighed. "I'll be like that woman with the beard who sells Jane Austen books at Camberwell Market."

"There's always Dodgy." Mira's lips were drawn in a smirk. "Most hookups happen in the workplace."

"Don't be dumb," I said. My hand went to my neck, a reflex to cover the rising blush. "Our relationship is strictly business."

Roger "Dodgy" Brick is my coworker at Videocity. We share the Sunday shift. Mira thinks he's hilarious, as in she likes to laugh *at* him not *with* him. He once tried to crack onto her by quoting from *Casablanca*. I can think of worse crimes. At least he knows his Spielbergs from his Soderberghs.

Now Mira amused herself by sifting through more

possibles for me: she mentioned several brother school castoffs; Mr. Pink, our chem teacher; Stanley, the "yoof" coordinator at Lo's father's parish; the creepy guy with the short-shorts and neck beard who replenished the school tuck-shop supplies, and the metalhead who worked in the meat section at Safeway.

"Oh, you're funny," I told her. "Really, you're killing me."

Lo was running her finger along a groove in the vinyl seat. She looked at me sideways. "I don't see why you need a boyfriend when you've got us."

"I love you, Lo, but I don't want to go out with you."

Lo bristled. "Why not?"

She wasn't serious! I knew she wasn't serious, but still my cheeks were burning up. After a few seconds of torment Lo's mask cracked.

"Oh please, Gem," she said sarcastically, "let me snuffle your truffles. Please!" She started to paw and tickle me. I shrieked, laughing, "Get off!"

"Bulldyke!" Mira blurted. She was laughing so hard Fanta came shooting out of her nose.

The sucker peers kept their eyes straight but Boobs stood up, with his face set on glare.

"Girls," he snapped, "control yourselves."

But it was too late for that. Lo pointed and yelped. Mira and I followed her finger. The vision of Boobs' disproportionately big arse in the fish-eye mirror sent us over the edge. Now we were in the land of stupid laughter— snorting and saliva spray. We laughed in rounds, until we were wrung out, hunched over, *hurting;* until I couldn't even remember how the laughter started.

It stopped soon enough. When we got off the bus, Mira and Lo went one way and I went the other. I couldn't help noticing that they walked with ease. They knew what it was like to be really, really liked. They not only had that knowledge, they had carnal knowledge too. I made a silent vow—I was going to join their ranks. Now all I needed was a target.

# *Dodgy Dealings*

I walked across the bridge and along the shopping strip, past the bakery, the post office, the candle shop, the secondhand book shop, and Inez Wisdom's Esoteric Emporium until I came to the squat beige cube that is my place of employment. Videocity's aesthetic is high scuzz: peeling paint, dated promo posters, rising damp, and dust motes. This is the place where videos come to die. There are miles of aisles bearing cases cracked and sun-bleached, with titles so Z-grade they should be outlawed. Not for nothing did Dodgy nickname the store Video Nasties.

I smoothed my hair and bit my lips to make them look redder, and then I opened the door. I was expecting to see Dodgy sitting with his back straight, watching something with subtitles and a soft jazz soundtrack; instead I walked into an aural landscape of screams and raining rubble. Marco, my other coworker, was sitting with his feet up on the counter. He was eating hot chips and watching *Earthquake* for the umpteenth time.

Marco and Dodgy are like different sides of the same coin. They're both doing film courses at TAFE—ostensibly so that they can access the equipment for free. Dodgy has a kind of slick appeal, but Marco has always reminded me of the cowardly lion in *The Wizard of Oz*. He has untamed hair, and pudge. His socks smell. He wants to growl, but for all his barbs, I could picture him saying affirmations in the mirror each morning. *You as much as anyone have the right to be loved . . .*

"Heya," he shouted over the din.

I covered my ears and mimed, "I can't hear you!"

He pressed the mute button.

"Thank you!" I stood back from the counter, maintaining a safe distance from his shoes. "What's going on?"

"Geneviève Bujold is about to fall into the canal." Marco gave a royal wave. "As you can see, I'm run off my feet."

The store was predictably empty. Wal, our boss, is a recluse and an anachronism. At the dawn of the DVD age, when all the outlying stores started offloading video stock, he went on a mad buying binge. He thought that Videocity would become Godhead for all suburban cinephiles. But they number below fifty—including the three already working for him. Lately Wal has let a few DVDs trickle through. He even had a sign made up: "NEW! DIGITAL VIDEO DISCS! SEE THE BIG SCREEN ON THE SMALL SCREEN!"

Wal is a marketing genius . . . not.

Video Nasties customers fall into two categories:

- The Lazy Locals—who can't be bothered to drive to Blockbuster and then get huffy when our one copy of *Anchorman* has already left the building
- The Old Faithfuls—a handful of regulars who can wax lyrical about Franz Waxman or Frank Thring or any other obscure film-related personality you could care to mention

Before I got the job at Video Nasties I was an Old Faithful. Only I didn't wax about anything. I just borrowed lots and lots, and I piqued Marco's interest, and he got me a work experience position there and I just kept turning up. Maybe I'm an anachronism too—maybe all Videocity employees are. Our film knowledge ranges far and wide and seems to expand backward. We each have our areas of interest: Marco cherishes disaster films, Dodgy is an expert on auteurs. I like old films; I am working my way through the eras. We all agree that anything post-1990 is just so much Schwarzenegger, although Marco has been known to sit through *The Day After Tomorrow*, for "educational" purposes.

"Is Dodgy here?" I asked Marco. I hoped my voice sounded innocent. I looked around just in case he was lurking.

"We swapped shifts," he said. He waited for me to say something else. I stepped over to the "Staff Recommends" shelf and started moving things around. I moved my *Chinatown* next to Dodgy's *Rififi*. I moved them so close their spines were touching.

"How come you want to see Dodgy?" Marco asked.

"I don't," I said. "I don't want to see him. I just came to get um, . . . this." I grabbed a video case and slid it along the counter. Marco looked at the case and then at me. The video was *The Sandpiper*, starring Elizabeth Taylor and Richard Burton. I picked it as mid-sixties but I'd never borrowed it before because it had a pink sticker that said "Ladies Choice." As the only female employee, I was careful to avoid anything too girly. Dodgy and Marco held a special measure of scorn for the chick flick.

"It's for my mum."

"Sure." Marco gave me a knowing smile. He picked up the remote. "Can I put this back on now?"

I nodded and went behind the counter, and plucked the tape from the file. The work roster was stuck on the side of the till. It read Dodgy, Dodgy, Dodgy—and it gave me an idea. Flirting one night a week wasn't going to get me anywhere; by the time the next Sunday rolled around, the days between would have wiped the slate clean. If I wanted to bring things up a belt notch with Dodgy, I was going to have to put in some overtime.

I tapped Marco on the shoulder. "Are there any shifts going next week? I can do days."

"There could be." Marco was always up for a day off. His official line was he needed to work less for 'the man' and more for himself, honing his 'craft'. Marco wrote treatments and film scripts. He was prolific, but unpro-duced.

"I've got study week," I explained.

"And . . . ?"

"And I thought I could bring my books in and . . . you know . . ."

"Earn while you learn?"

"Exactly." I gave him a wide smile.

He picked up the roster. "You can do Wednesday," he said. "And if you promise to plague Dodgy with Julia Roberts vehicles, you can have Friday too."

"Done." I shook his hand.

"Now, is there anything else?" he asked. "Because I'm trying to watch this fine example of eschatological cinema."

"That's a big word." I grabbed a handful of his chips, and popped them into my mouth.

"Nice," he commented. "Eat my dinner, why don't you?"

"Dodgy's still working with me on Sunday, right?"

"Er, yes." Marco gave me a quizzical look. "You know, you're talking about Dodgy *a lot*."

"Am I?" I hugged *The Sandpiper* to my chest and made steps toward the door. Marco almost followed through, but on-screen the aftershocks kept coming, the Capitol building was set to crumble, Charlton Heston was looking stressed; what was my mini-drama compared to all that carnage?

# Boho Bev

When I got home, Bev was stirring bouillabaisse with one hand and punching through her slide show on the Impressionists with the other. I dropped my bag with a thud and leaned against the bench. I waited for her to acknowledge me—she didn't—so after a few more seconds of silence I asked myself, "Hi chook, how was school?"

My cultivated moron voice replied, "It didn't completely suck."

"I'll just be a sec," Bev said, still with her back to me. She clicked a button and a Parisian street scene curled around the edges of the window blind.

I plucked our copy of the *I Ching* from its home atop the bread bin. It's a fat book based on an ancient Taoist system of divination. Purists use coins or yarrow sticks to find the hexagram that will give them the answer to their big what-if. Bev and I prefer the cheat's route: we ask the question, then open the book onto a random page and let our index finger fall on the answer. Sometimes we bypass the question altogether. Like now. I flipped the book open, closed my eyes, and dowsed my finger over the page.

Bev turned around. Her face was red from stove heat. She blew upward to get her fringe off her eyes. She looked a little tired, but pleased to see me. "What did you get?"

I looked at the text underneath my fingertip.

*"Misfortune comes to he who wears the cloak of perpetual restlessness."*

"Hmm." Bev went into a deep think. Her brow furrowed as she burrowed in the fridge. She brought out a bottle of cranberry juice and poured us both a glass. I drank mine in three quick swigs. When I came up for air, I saw Bev regarding me seriously.

"What?" I asked.

She peered and probed. "Are you restless, honey?"

My mother is more left than right. Insisting I call her by her first name is just the tip of the iceberg. For a long time I didn't know Bev was different from other mothers. I ignored the signs: sunflower seeds in my lunch; the *Green Left* on the coffee table; petitions, protests, peripatetic friends; fear of fast food, antibiotics, and things not made by hand. This stuff adds up.

Recognition hit the day Mira wangled me an invitation to go swimming at Bliss Dartford's house. This was back in year eight—when I still cared. That day I bobbed around the deep end, hiding my unfashionable one-piece, imagining how life could be. I was almost there. And then Bev came to pick me up wearing *that* T-shirt, decades-thin, boldly proclaiming Germaine Greer's slogan in bold type—"Lady love your —— "

Well I hate to be *blunt*, but that's what it rhymes with.

Now I wish she'd been wearing it for show, but the truth was less inciting. Bev had come straight from working on a sculpture—and when she was slapping clay, her wardrobe was immaterial. So, she was wearing the T-shirt, and Bliss Dartford's mother went white, and all us kids had a new word on our vocab lists that week.

Lo loves this story. She wants to take the T-shirt out of retirement. I know that Bev keeps it on the back of her bedroom door. But I associate it with crying and confusion and Bliss Dartford's evil even-toothed smile.

Where we live it doesn't take much to stand out. It's a little bit country and not at all rock 'n' roll. My mother grew up here. Her story is that when she was my age, all she wanted to do was leave. And she did . . . but then she came back.

"So why did you come back?" I used to ask her, hugging myself because I knew the answer.

She'd chuck me under the chin and say, "Because I had you."

This was my cue to lay the back of my hand on my brow. "Are you saying I stole you away from an extraordinary life?"

And Bev would give me her special look of Tender

Motherly Love. "No, chook, I'm saying you gave me my home."

Bev likes to say I am her work-in-progress, but I think her masterpiece resides on the back porch. It is a *papier-mâché* sculpture she calls *Magic Man*. Lo says the effigy is Bev's emotional deposit box—like if he came to life, he'd know every little thing about her—but I'd rather see her romancing her own creation than some septuagenarian swinger with a hot car and a hairpiece.

That awful period when Bev turned to Internet dating resulted in a parade of unsuitable father figures. I dreaded the Sunday lunch and look-over. The last one nearly did her in. His username was Don JB. He was short and fond of saying, "It's ironical." Bev went out with him for two months, had sex with him—everything—then he told her he was married. I found her at four in the morning, crying into the *I Ching*. She didn't even like him, she said. She was having a delayed adolescence. Then she went back online under a different username to catch him out.

Bev and I have a rapport, but there are some things I don't tell her. Like how I was glad things didn't work out with Don JB. And not just in a churlish "If I can't get any, I don't see why she should" way. Bev has always said we're okay, just the two of us, and I really want to believe it's true.

# Brain Trees

While the bouillabaisse bubbled away, I went online in search of the perfect Ug guide. I was looking for someone not too obscure, but not too obvious. Someone arch and impressible. I wanted to rock up to HQ and say the magic name and see Lo's smile clear through her cigarette smoke.

I typed in "Underground," "Bohemian," "Decadent," and "Avant-Garde." I cruised olde worlde literary sites and maps for the Czech Republic. There was a bunch of stuff about the beats, but Jack Kerouac lived with his mother, and I was already doing that. The sites for "avant-garde" were a minefield of -isms; negative space, dancers who danced to no music, musicians who played only silence, a lot of words I needed a dictionary for. "Decadent" threw up porn (will Bev never childproof this rig?). I sampled some goth erotica, and just when my face couldn't get any redder, my mother came nosin' around.

"What are you looking at, chook?"

I clicked the minimiser and crossed my legs. "Just study . . . stuff."

Then it struck me that Bev, fervent believer in the bizarre choice, could make mine for me. I followed her into the kitchen.

"We need to brainstorm," I told her. "I'm going to say a word—you say the first thing that comes into your head. But it has to be a person. Okay?"

She nodded, the eager beaver. She loves association games.

"Underground," I barked.

"*The Hobbit*," Bev returned like a game-show queen.

I made the wrong buzzer noise. "A *real* person."

"Oh, oh!" She snapped her fingers. "Saddam Hussein?"

I shook my head. "It has to be someone admirable. Ready? Underground!"

"Abbie Hoffman!"

I'd heard this name somewhere before. "Who's he again?"

Bev looked pleased with herself. "He was a counterculture rebel in the sixties."

I paused. "Was he a hippie? I don't want any hippies."

I believe there is something suss and mung-beanish

about hippies, something slow and sodden. This is because of my father.

. . .

Bev's ancient photo albums reveal that Rolf Gordon, my father, had a Fu Manchu moustache and frizzy hair. He favoured denim jeans and hemp hairshirts. He knocked Bev up and then lit out for the Tasmanian wilderness, where he still lives and works today as a park ranger. Bev would never say she planned it, but she thrives on being a one-woman parental unit—this way it's like she invented me all on her own. Frankenstein, anyone?

She insists that she wasn't heartbroken over his defection, but I suspect she still has a candle burning for him somewhere. How else do you explain her lack of romantic action since? Bev says that time has rendered Rolf into something sweet and abstract; for me he's something else altogether. I used to dream about standing at the foot of the mountain, setting it alight, and smoking him out, caveman style. Now I just shrug. When people ask about him I always say, "He's out of the picture," like he's some movie extra cut from the crowd scene. The truth is I don't know what to think about him. I bypass the question.

Rolf is not completely out of sight, out of mind. He sends us "contemporary" haikus for Christmas and birthdays. They're sucky, and they make no sense.

*The cub faces the Yaw*
*His chest hurts with courage*
*The Yaw has teeth that close together*

Bev was starting to look distracted. I snapped my fingers trying to bring her back. "Underground!"

"What's this for anyway?" Bev asked. She picked up the projector button and jiggled it in her hand. *Click:* Monet's *Waterlilies. Click:* Manet's naked lady on the picnic rug.

"It's a project—something that me and Lo and Mira are doing for the summer. I need a guide to inspire me." I remembered something Lo had said: "I'm trying to broaden my cultural horizons."

"Who's Lo doing?"

My mother loves Lo. *Loves* her. Whenever they're around each other, their voices start to meld. I'm not sure if Lo's faking, if it's all Art for Bev's sake, but whatever they're discussing, Capitals are applied and syllables are *stressed*. Every little thing is awash with meaning. Um . . . annoying much?

"I don't know who Lo's doing," I snapped. Game over.

Bev started opening drawers and cupboard doors, taking out plates and cutlery. This was my cue to set the table. But I just sat there, scowling, feeling like a dullard.

Bev sighed. "What's the matter with you?" She grabbed my hand, flipped it palm up, and dug her thumb into a pressure point. "Are you worried about exams?"

I shook my head. I could handle exams. I was worried about finding a guide. I didn't want Lo to come up with one for me. Lo always got the good ideas first. Her father published a Christian e-bulletin, cringingly called *The New Dawn*, and Lo's access to his home office—computer, printers, copiers, fax machine, broadband—made her a wellspring of weird information.

Bev kept kneading. "Did you have a good time at the gallery?" she asked.

"It was . . . interesting," I said. "Boobs told us that art was like a psychic mirror. But he didn't tell us what a psychic mirror was."

"Oh. He just means when you look at something and it seems to reflect what you're feeling on the inside." Bev dug between my pinky and ring fingers, adding, "I really wish you'd find another nickname for him, he can't help it if he has a weight problem."

"I saw this cool installation," I said. "TV screens showing close-ups of people kissing. Black and white."

"Ahhh, Warhol," Bev said like he was an old friend. She pushed down on my pressure point with more intensity. "Why don't you use him for your project?"

I thought about it. "Isn't pop art like 'art lite'?"

"Hardly." Bev moved into teacher mode. "Pop art was a slap in the face of abstract expressionism. Warhol turned western consumerism in on itself. You don't know this?"

"I know that in the future everyone will be famous for fifteen minutes," I rattled off.

"I say Warhol, you think reality TV. Sometimes I feel sorry for your generation. Irony is a curse. Pointless things are made out to be important. Real art gets diluted . . ." Now Bev was pulling on my skin, practically giving me webbed fingers. "Am I supposed to sit idly by while society dumbs my daughter down?"

"Ow!" I yanked my hand away. "I'm not that bad." I smiled, twisty and teasing, "I could be so much worse. *Like, Omigod!*" I transformed myself into the ditzy daughter of my mother's nightmares. Overuse of the L-word is one of my mother's pet peeves. She also has a problem with G-strings, tongue piercing, rampant depilation, butt cleavage, the resurrection of David Hasselhoff, and T-shirts with slogans like "bitch" and "foxy."

"Oohhh!" Bev put me in a headlock and laughed her "evil" laugh. She looked over her shoulder and nodded to the clattering saucepan lid. "That's ready."

. . .

During dinner, a warm breeze snuck through the kitchen window. Bev kept the lights low, and Van Gogh's *Starry Night* swirled and wobbled on the blind, our backdrop.

"It's beautiful." Bev came over all dreamy. "Each successive stroke of paint carries the weight of its predecessor."

"It's like brain trees," I told her.

"What are brain trees?"

"They're like mind maps. We do them in English for

creative bloodletting. You know, each branch is a thought that leads to the next branch and so on." I waved my spoon like a wand. "But you can never get back to that first thought."

"Ahhh." Bev shook her head and smiled and let me think I was the sage one.

· · ·

That night as I lay in bed, my brain tree was a gnarled cypress. My thoughts backed over themselves. Andy Warhol and Lo and my father all featured. But mostly I thought about Bev. My mother—the cook, art critic, and philosopher—wore her heart on her sleeve and all her hats at once. I had a sneaking suspicion that all my branches led back to her.

# The Warhol Look

Friday was the last official school day before study week. It was also a designated free-dress day, the perfect opportunity for Mira, Lo, and I to parade our new Ug-ness. I woke early, feeling ringy with anticipation. Outside summer was percolating. I knew there was nothing revolutionary about cargo shorts and a T-shirt, so I made a beeline for Bev's bedroom. My mother is a pack rat. The upside to this is that she still has all her crazy clothes from decades past. People say you turn into your mother, and I remember an article in *Marie Claire* where mother and daughter teams leotarded up and marvelled over their similarities. But Bev is a little teapot, short and stout, and I am a beanpole.

I had to push through a mountain of crochet before I found my dream dress: it was a simple brown shift, edged with tiny felt roses. I wore a black vest underneath it so no one could clock my nubs through the armholes.

Unfortunately the only summer shoes I had were my orthopaedic sandals, so I opted for socks and work boots. My reflection in the hallway mirror (which doesn't get much natural light) showed a peasant girl from a fifties film by a European director. Perfect! I put on Yum-Yum Plum lip balm, tied my hair up in two bunches, and sauntered out to the kitchen.

Bev looked up from her coffee. "What's his name?"

"Please!" I scoffed. "I have far more important things on my agenda."

Bev's eyebrows pointed to the skylight. I could tell she was secretly proud. She hates girls who get all gaga over guys. She thinks the reason I don't have a boyfriend is because I'm particular. Ha-ha.

I sat down opposite her and started scoffing Vegemite toast.

"So, it's your last day," Bev observed, "and you've been working hard . . ." She produced a neatly wrapped present from behind her back. "I got you something."

The card was a picture of Andy Warhol and "It" girl icon Edie Sedgwick, posing in a manhole on a New York street. On the reverse Bev had written, "For your project!" I dusted off my fingers and tore into the raffia until my fingers revealed a book—a coffee-table tome called *The Warhol Look*.

"Wow! It's great. Thank you."

"Well, I'm proud of you." Bev beamed. "Should I hang on to it until after exams? I don't want you getting distracted."

"I won't get distracted," I told her. I looked down quickly so she wouldn't see the "guilty" light flashing on my forehead. It was true that I'd spent the last two days in front of the computer. But I'd been cramming for Ug, not for exams. Instead of getting my English quotes in order I'd been Googling Andy Warhol, preparing my case for Lo and Mira. I'd learned that Warhol and his "Superstars" lived artistically. His workspace—dubbed the Factory— was like a drop-in centre: film stars, trannies, debs, and druggies all rubbed up against each other inside its silver-foiled walls. Warhol recorded everything from the banal to the bizarre. I loved that idea, even if the reality of it was impractical.

I opened the book and stared at the beautiful, the jaded, the wrecked, and the vacant. Edie Sedgwick looked so hip in her black tights, dancing with her eyes closed, her head tucked down, her foot angled just so. She looked like she didn't care about anyone, but everyone cared about her. I wanted a bit of that allure.

Maybe I had it. I could feel Bev gazing at me. I glanced up.

"You look pretty," she said.

I made a face and took another piece of toast. Bev could go from cool to corny in the flutter of an eyelid. Sometimes I wished she were less emotional. Sometimes when she stared at me like that, it was hard not to feel like a specimen. I turned the pages and said, "I know you're still looking, I can feel it."

"I just . . . I can't believe you're almost grown."

"I know," I said tartly, "I'm practically an adult."

When she didn't laugh I looked up. She was hiding behind her coffee mug. "Are you crying?" I asked her.

"It's the change," she squeaked.

I smiled. "You always say that."

And then she ambushed me with a hug. She smelled like sleep and sandalwood, and I held on longer than I thought I would.

. . .

HQ, 8:30 a.m.

Lo was wearing bumster jeans and a top she'd created with two silk scarves. She had on masses of eyeliner, gypsy hoop earrings, and another scarf pulled over her forehead. Mira was wearing tight blank pants with a green army shirt. Instead of carrying her books in her backpack she had an old wooden basket.

We air-kissed hellos, and they did their routine.

"Sniff the air," Mira urged, "it's full of promise."

"Cigarette smoke more like," Lo drawled.

She looked me up and down. "You look cool," she noted. Then she turned to the mirror and checked herself out. "I've been getting crazy ideas for Ug."

"Like what?" Mira asked.

Lo smiled mysteriously. "You'll see . . ."

I felt a small tremor of excitement. Mira winced. "The last time you had a crazy idea, my car ended up in the river."

Mira was referring to the time when Lo had an "emergency" involving a rendezvous with an anonymous male. She borrowed Mira's sixteenth-birthday present—a sweet little Fiat—and got bogged in river mud. We're still not sure what happened—something to do with the handbrake was all Lo said.

"What's the point of having a car when you can't even drive?" Lo asked.

"I *can* drive," Mira said.

"Yeah, but you have to have your mother with you."

"Or any licensed driver," Mira retorted.

"Your mother!" Lo coughed into her hand.

I watched the two of them locked in combat, staring each other down to see who would crack up first. And it reminded me of something I didn't like to think about: that all year Lo and Mira had been moving closer and closer together. We three weren't as equal as I wanted us to be.

"Hey ladies," I called out. "Break it up."

Mira stuck her tongue out at Lo. Lo blinked and smiled stupidly. Then she linked her arm through mine. "What about Gem-Gem? Have you got any crazy ideas for us?"

I twisted my foot inward. I could feel the weight of the book in my bag. Now was my moment to blurt "Andy Warhol! Andy Warhol!" but I paused. The bell was about to ring. Lo was preoccupied with adjusting her scarves and Mira had disappeared into a stall. Andy deserved a bigger entrance than that.

So instead of answering, I told Lo she looked dead

witchy with all that eyeliner, and she pulled the pencil out of her bag and did my eyes, then Mira's. We marched through the school gates and thumbed our collective nose at the sucker peers, who were all wearing Jeans West bar code fodder and looked like absolute kids. Bliss Dartford and Ponyface Roberts were sitting on a bench, blending into each other in their pastel hues.

Lo nodded to them. "Piss, Pony."

Mira walked by with her head high. I was proud of her.

Bliss sneered, "What are you supposed to be?" and Pony said, "Freak Faction at ten o'clock." But there was something else behind their eyes—a grudging respect. And then a year-eight girl took a photo of us with her phone, and it was obvious to all and sundry that we were officially too cool for school.

# Pascal's Wager

We didn't have proper classes that day, just lectures about study guides and how to battle exam nerves. We all had to go in and see the school counsellor, Ms. Sharon Minski, for a pep talk.

Sharon Minski is hovering around the mid-forties, and built like a little Buddha. Her skin is tough and freckly. Her rusty red hair has a bum part. She favours too-bright clothes from third world countries. She has a hundred and one sponsor children, and as such her office is littered with portraits and thank-yous like Vietnamese wall hangings, Guatemalan worry dolls, and Ethiopian tribal masks.

Sharon plays a dual role in my life. She may be the school counsellor, but she is also my godmother. She and my mother were at Melbourne Uni back in the days when anyone could afford to go there, and they are like *that*. I find it hard to maintain an antiauthoritarian stance around Sharon. Lo and Mira have no such problem—they call her the Mince or Mincy, and call my credibility into question. Sharon's no fairy godmother; there's no trust fund and no wand to magick away my troubles. She's big on giving books: "Beyond your years, to keep you edgy." But I don't know. This birthday I got *Notes from Underground* by Fyodor Dostoevsky. The introduction says it's about tragedy and deformity and self-torture. These concepts are not foreign to the average teenager.

To university or not to university? That is the question.

Lo scoffs at higher education. She's not even sure if she'll go on to year twelve. And Mira doesn't think tertiary. She'll be lucky if she passes this year. They say I can be their representative in the straight world, but I'm hoping there's something in between. At my last session with Sharon I made a mumble about film school. She didn't say "Pardon?" She didn't say anything.

.   .   .

"So how's that *Magic Man* coming along?" Sharon asked. She was grinning like a sheepdog. "Hard to believe it's been a year."

"He's got killer abs," I told her. "But he still lacks a face."

"She's a true artist, your mother."

Sharon is always crapping on about Bev's "genius." When she says stuff like this, I often get the urge to blow her a big juicy raspberry. Not to disrespect my mother, but if she's such a "true artist," why is she stuck at the local Community Centre teaching house-wives how to make mandalas out of bicycle wheels and alpaca wool? Bev says it's not about the end; it's about "the journey." But that sounds like a line—what people say when their future turns out to be something they didn't sign up for.

I concentrated on the manila folder on Sharon's desk in an effort to bring the light back on me.

"Right. Film school." She brought out a brochure. "The Film & Television College is competitive. They only accept a small percentage of school leavers. They like you to have a bit of life experience."

"Naturally." My smile was tight. "All *great artists* draw on life experience."

Sharon ignored my dig. "You need a show reel—have you got a show reel?"

"Um . . . ," I opened my mouth and closed it again. Guppy Gem.

"How about a backup plan?"

I stared at her. "How about if you don't have a backup plan you can't fall back?"

She held her sides, pretended to laugh. Then she asked me, "Have you heard of Pascal's wager?"

"No." I shifted in my seat.

Sharon said, "Pascal was a French polymath in the sev-enteenth century. He said that in a world of uncertainty, believing in God was the safest bet. Then if it turns out that He exists, you get eternal reward. And if you're wrong, the worst case scenario is that you die, *boom*, everything goes black, and you've only wasted a few thousand hours in prayer. Go the other way . . ." Sharon raised a finger to stifle my oncoming groan. "Go the other way, and you'll suffer eternal damnation."

"I thought you were an atheist," I said.

"That's not my point. I'm saying be smart. Keep your options open."

"You want me to go to Melbourne Uni and do arts. You want me to be a sheep."

Sharon gave me a look.

"You do. You and Mum."

"Gem, have you even looked at the course guide? An arts degree can incorporate media studies, cinema studies."

"Yeah, yeah," I grumbled. I had no good argument against Melbourne. I just didn't want to have to think about it *now*. Why couldn't I be a contrary Mary? Outside the window, students were settling down to lunch in the sunshine. Maybe I just didn't want to do what was expected of me.

Sharon made a church steeple with her fingers. "You can always defer. Take a semester off, get a job, go fruit picking, do a farm stay—what do they call it? Woofing. Whatever you kids do these days . . ."

Woofing!

I picked up the FTC brochure and gave it a good hard look. On it a goateed guy viewed the world through the rectangle of his joined thumbs and forefingers. I kicked my foot against the desk leg, one, two, three dull thuds. I felt a sudden clutch of yearning. Was he a true artist, or was he just having a shot? Did he have a show reel? Meanwhile, Sharon was looking at me with a mixture of pity and impatience.

"That was the bell," she hinted.

.  .  .

I was walking back to the common room when the idea hit me. Suddenly it was as if the sun was shining directly on me. My world went from monochrome to technicolour. I had a goal for Ug and it was absolute genius.

School finished early with a barbecue prepared by the year nines—hello salmonella! Me and my underground comrades blew that off and hopped the city train. For the forty-minute ride we barely spoke, each in our own private headspaces. Back fences choked by morning glory tumbled past. Fat families got on, hoodlums got off. An old man behind us repeated the announcements word-perfect. With each stop the graffiti grew more sophisticated. Soon the houses were smaller, brickier, and there was little green to be seen. When the city buildings cast a shadow through the train window, it was shaped like teeth.

# A Cool Artist Thing

The city was gearing up for high Friday-night fever. Me, Lo, and Mira walked up Swanston Street past sparking trams and sullen taxi drivers. We shouted at each other over barkers and the unholy *crash-bang* of the Hare Krishnas. When we got to the State Library, we parked on the stone steps and did a spot of people watching. Couples lolled on the lawn; skater kids turned tricks or came off their boards with a spit and a shrug. A steady stream thronged into Melbourne Central: IT guys, PR women, students, our non-bar code brethren—cute boys in AC/DC T-shirts, cool girls in stripy tights, red lipstick, and lethal black boots. We breathed it all in. Lo was grinning. "There's no place like home."

. . .

The State Library is one of my favourite places because it's free to get into and filled with the perfume of knowledge. Mira finds it a challenge because it's rife with nerd boys. Lo knows every inch of it; she did work experience in the newspaper annexe. She is Our Lady of the Microfiche.

We entered the cool marble foyer, checked our bags with the Papa Bear security guard, clutched our folders, and walked directly to the big staircase at the end of the building. Upstairs, we found our favourite secret corral. Lo sat first—this was her talk show—Mira and I sat to her left. She took out her spiral-bound notebook and smoothed her hand over a blank page.

"So. We're here to discuss Underground Summer, aka Ug."

"Ug-ug!" Mira shimmied her shoulders.

Lo stared her down. "Don't do that anymore."

"Sorry."

Lo meant business. All the drama was making me nervous. I had *The Warhol Look* hidden in my folder, my own little Ug bomb ready to blow.

Lo said, "I think this year we should have a shared goal—a united front—a big picture—"

"I know what that is." Mira grabbed Lo's pen and drew a wonky penis. Lo looked down. "Thanks for that." She turned the page over and started again. "This might be our sunset. Who knows where we'll be next year. We might not even be in the same *country*. So we should, you know, make the most of it."

I made an involuntary squeak of excitement.

Lo spread her palms across the table. "Gem, have you got any thoughts?" Her mouth twitched. "No dickering."

I had. I did. I couldn't believe I'd managed to contain my genius for this long. I leaned forward, straight in. "I want to make a movie, an underground movie."

Lo and Mira sat silent as stones. Like I'd just told them I wanted to spend the summer slaughtering babies. Neither of them was expecting me to have an idea. There was no precedent for this kind of initiative. Mira's eyes were big and round behind her specs. She wasn't going to say anything unless Lo did. Lo was chewing her pen, blue ink leaking onto her lips. She was wearing her poker face. She could go either way.

I said, "So I had my session with Sharon and she was all, "the Film and Television College is super-selective" and "don't put all your eggs in one basket" and it just came to me—*make a film*. Like, why wait when I'm ready now? I mean, how hard can it be? Camera, script, actors." I zipped it before the list could overwhelm us.

Lo looked constipated, or should I say trumped? This was a first. I felt a little tickle of triumph and then immediately felt guilty. Until then I hadn't known I was trying to show her up.

After what felt like an age she put her pen down and spat a gob of blue into her hand. "I like it," she said. "An underground film for our Underground Summer."

"Okay." Mira's bottom lip jutted out. "What's an underground film?"

Lo looked at me.

"Um, the opposite of Hollywood." I scrambled around for a better definition. "Non-mainstream, experimental . . . Like the film at the gallery. The kissing one, remember?"

Mira nodded and then shook her head. A yes-no was the best we could expect from her until all the information had sunk in.

Lo gave me a nod. "I'll be producer, you can direct."

"What about me? What'll I do?" Mira asked.

I made the rectangle with my fingers and viewed Mira's worried mug through it.

"Annnnd action!" I said.

Mira struck a pose. We all smiled. Lo's teeth were stained blue. Now I plonked *The Warhol Look* on the table and told them, "I've already thought of a guide—Andy Warhol."

"Wow." Lo clicked her jaw. "You've been busy. You're not the only one with ideas, you know." Her voice was light, but she wouldn't look at me. I decided to play the diplomat. It wouldn't do to steal *all* her thunder.

"Sorry," I said. "What's your idea?"

Lo pulled a piece of paper out of her jeans pocket. Under an image of a teenage girl tearing her hair out, the text read:

NEW YEAR'S EVE. FOURTEEN DEAD. "There was blood everywhere!" says local teen. "One minute Jimmy was standing there holding my hand, and the next I was still holding his hand, but the rest of him was in pieces all over the ground!"

"What is it?" I asked.

"It's Art Terrorism," Lo said, like it was obvious. Then she grinned. "I guess the gallery got me too."

My first reaction was one of derision. I was thinking "Where's the art?" but it wouldn't do to dismiss Lo's effort so quickly. I tried to think philosophically. This was pure Lo; she wasn't happy unless she was upending the world. This was the difference between us—I wanted to make things, Lo wanted to break things. Ordinarily I wouldn't fight it, but not this time. This time my idea was better.

"I don't get it," Mira said finally. "Is it like a chain letter?"

"It's Art Terrorism," Lo said again through gritted teeth. "We put it up around town and people get freaked."

"That's it?"

Lo stared at me. This was her talk show and I was like the rebel guest who'd spurned the autocue.

"Don't you think the blood stuff's a bit OTT?" I asked.

"O-kay . . ." Lo sucked her breath back. And then the unthinkable occurred—another first in a day of firsts—Lo backpedaled. "It doesn't have to be this . . . *specifically*," she said. "I just thought it'd be fun to put it out there— like a flyer."

"Yeah, a flyer's cool." I had to give her something.

Now silence drew a bow between us. Mira's head wobbled.

Lo started slowly. "Flyers are easy. Dad just bought a monster photocopier. What if . . ." she was getting warmer, ". . . we make a film and screen it at an underground party."

Suddenly I got it. "A Happening!" I almost shouted.

"Huh?" That was Mira.

"A Happening. A cool artist thing. It would be totally Ug. Andy Warhol used to have them."

Lo said, "See? We're on the same page." But she smiled too quickly. Her eyes were streets behind, dark with other ideas. "We could totally commandeer New Year's."

The local council has an annual party at the river reserve for New Year's Eve. It's a family affair and underagers forced to attend *will* unleash their inner delinquent. There's usually a Ferris wheel and fireworks. Grape growers from the valley storm the Community Centre. The organic wine flows freely.

"We could show the film there!" I clapped my hands together. "On a big screen—like a guerrilla screening!"

"What—like monkeys?" Mira asked.

She was ignored.

Lo nodded, and scratched her pen across paper.

"So what happens at a Happening?" Mira wanted to know.

"Cocaine, canapés, light shows, Superstars." I was only half-joking. I pushed *The Warhol Look* under Mira's nose.

"Who's she?" Mira asked. She had her finger on Edie Sedgwick. Edie with her white-blonde hair and leopard-skin coat, immaculately made-up, cigarette at the ready. Cool and crazy.

"She was Andy's muse," I said. "She had a trust fund and a speed habit. She starred in his films. She used to dance and dance and she only travelled by limousine." I turned the page to a party scene. "Andy Warhol had a Factory where he did all his art," I told them. "He had an open-door policy, and all sorts of crazy people would turn up and never leave. This guy here used to sleep in the toilet. He covered the whole Factory in silver foil."

"Cool," Mira said. "It looks like a rave."

"Oh no, it was much more than that," I said.

Lo looked up. She reached over and removed Mira's glasses. Then she turned to me. "What do you think?"

I held Mira's jaw and studied her. Her face was open, if a little confused. "We start with a close-up, then pan back." I re-angled her head, like I imagined a real director would.

"What am I doing?" Mira pressed her jaw into my palm. Her eyes raced around the room.

I said, "That, my friend, is what we've got to work out."

Mira and I opened our notebooks to copy down what Lo had written:

GEM TO DIRECT UG FILM
LO-PRODUCER

MIRA-SUPERSTAR
ANDY WARHOL
EDIE SEDGWICK
HAPPENING
ART TERROR
NEW YEAR'S EVE BIG SCREEN

Lo closed her notebook. "We need a camera. And we need to research."

I said, "We should each try and come up with a script."

"Reconvene next week," Lo said. "Wednesday?"

"I'm working," I said. Phase one of my Dodgy attack.

"Tuesday then." She glanced at Mira's notebook. Mira had stopped copying at "Superstar." The rest of the page was just doodles and her name in bubble print over and over.

"Mira!" Lo rapped her knuckles on the table.

Mira blinked like someone had just turned the lights on and said, "Mincy told me I should do summer school. I'm like, 'Do I look retarded?'" She dropped her jaw and made a spazzy sound.

I rubbed her arm. But it was hard to feel sorry for her. For one thing I was all excited about Ug, and for another—to use the parlance of the olds—Mira didn't exactly apply herself.

"Mincy wants my parents in for a powwow." Mira turned to me with a power pout. "Can't you do anything?"

"Sharon doesn't listen to me," I told her.

"But you are *so* Mincy's minion."

Mira looked to Lo for backup, but Lo had moved on. She was hmm-ing and haa-ing, nutting out the logistics of our grand new goal. "What we really need," she said, "is a Factory."

# *Ladies Choice*

Inez Wisdom says the way to remember your dreams is to drink half a glass of water before you go to sleep and then finish the glass first thing in the morning. When I woke up on Saturday I took the prompt, and sure enough, as the water went down, my dream bubbled back up. I'd been hoping for something romantic—a portent of things to come. What I got was me, Lo, and Mira playing skipping games in the school quadrangle. Mira and Lo were holding the ends, and I was doing the jumping. Only I was all out of sync, and Lo and Mira were laughing and turning the ropes faster and faster. This much I knew: I was going to fall, and when I did, it was going to hurt.

The dream coloured the rest of my day. Every time I thought about my friends, I felt uneasy. I even resisted the urge to work on my Ug script in favour of proper study. Somehow it felt safer.

At five o'clock Bev came home from her alpaca wool sessions and knocked on my door. "What are we watching tonight?"

"Something romantic," I said. "*The Sandpiper*—it's 'ladies' choice."

"Should I dress up?"

"Yeah!" I put on my dirty old man voice. "Wear something pretty for me."

But Bev wasn't joking. When I went upstairs she was faffing around the kitchen in her old kimono and a red feather boa. Her hair was piled on top of her head. She wore lipstick and had even drawn on a beauty spot. She looked at my shorts and T-shirt in dismay. "You used to love dressing up."

"When I was twelve."

Bev's face went pink. I hadn't meant to sound so harsh. I tried to soften the blow by crossing my arms over my attire. "But now I feel so frumpy!" I wailed.

Bev raised her eyebrows. "Here." She unwound the boa and draped it around my neck. "You could have at least put some lipstick on." She shook her head. "Go on, use mine. It's in the bathroom."

We sat on the couch in our matching lipstick opposite a big plate of nachos and a pitcher of nonalcoholic martinis. *The Sandpiper* was in the machine and ready to go.

Bev held her glass high. "To Saturday night!"

I clinked it. "To Romance!"

We exchanged sad-puppy faces, turned out the light, and settled back to the strains of strings.

. . .

A good movie partner is hard to find. Lo's a snorter—she has trouble with the whole suspension-of-disbelief thing. Mira is a gas-bagger—she starts asking questions from the opening credits. Dodgy and Marco tend to overintellectualise every little detail. Only Bev seems to understand how much I want to be transported. We have a strict no-talking policy, but there were moments in *The Sandpiper* that were so close to home, it was all I could do to not jab her in the ribs.

In the film, Elizabeth Taylor plays a "lady artist" who lives with her son in a bohemian beach shack. They paint watercolours and read Chaucer for kicks, but then her son gets into trouble, and Liz is forced to send him to a religious school. Richard Burton is the principal of the school. Right from the first, he and Liz have frisson. They fight about man and God and the role of women in society—and then they fold into an embrace against the crashing shoreline. Ultimately, Richard Burton's guilt gets the better of him; Eva Marie Saint, his nunlike wife, gets sniffy; and Liz Taylor returns to her shack, sadder and wiser and still so beautiful.

*The Sandpiper* featured dodgy hairdos, a range of glittering caftans, and Charles Bronson playing a beatnik sculptor. And even though Liz Taylor was a bit pissy, and

Richard Burton was a bit shouty, when it was all over I felt struck with melancholy.

"It never would have worked," I said, hugging my cushion.

"Love is a cage." Bev's face was grave. "That's the moral of the story. Like the sandpiper, Liz had to be free."

"Remind you of anyone?" I asked. I meant Bev, of course. I thought she'd smile, but she just looked at me blankly. She'd polished off her martini and was now nibbling on the olive.

"What's that, darling?"

"Single mother, lady artist, funky house." I scanned our living room. It was full of Bev's artifacts and knick-knackery. "I mean, they could have filmed it here," I said. "Look—driftwood, sculpture, still life with kiwi fruit . . ."

Now she laughed. "Oh, sure! I think I would have stuck with Charles Bronson, though. Richard Burton was much too uptight."

"So, how many stars would you give it?" I asked her. "Leonard Maltin only gave it two and a half."

Bev thought about it. "Three. One for the scenery, one for Liz's wardrobe, and one for the fact that they referenced Thoreau."

"I give it a three too," I decided. "Who's Thoreau?"

Bev's face got the hippie taint. She quoted, "The mass of men lead lives of quiet desperation." She presented her palms like Jesus displaying his wounds. She often did this when trying to indicate genius or hopelessness. Then she got up, went over to the bookshelf, and took out a paperback. She handed it to me.

"That was your father's bible."

*Walden* by Henry David Thoreau. The book was bumped and scuffed. I tried to read the back cover but something else was taking over. Considering the minor role he played in my life, my father seemed to be getting an awful lot of publicity.

"Bev?"

"Mmm-hmm?"

"You know how Liz Taylor said she didn't want to get married because then she'd lose part of herself?"

"Yessss?"

"Was it like that for you?"

Bev looked at me, surprised.

"Like how she said—women only get to be wives and mothers, but men get to be whatever they want?"

"Those were different times," Bev said. "I'm not that old!"

"You know what I mean."

She hesitated, and then said, "Getting married wasn't the important thing. Your father . . ." She broke off. She looked like she couldn't find the words. ". . . didn't do things by numbers. But him leaving—that was a mutual decision."

I wasn't sure I believed her. *Mutual* was a word that sucker peers used when brother school boys had reeled them in, and then tossed them back. It sounded so passionless, so non-Bev, so . . . *democratic*. I wanted my father's leaving to be all her idea; because if it was his, then I wasn't sure what that made me. Except unwanted.

Bev's eyes wandered down to my hands, still gripping *Walden*. "You should read that." I couldn't believe she was trying to change the subject. Was that it! I looked down at the book and threw her the peace sign with a sarcastic smile. Then Bev reached for my fingers and clasped them in hers. She said, "I'm sorry, chook, it's just . . . you never ask about him. I wasn't ready for it. Let's start again. Ask me something, anything you want."

"I wasn't asking about *him*," I rushed back. "I was asking about you." My eyes felt hot. I felt like I'd been caught out. Bev was looking at me like I was an endangered species.

I stood up. "You know what? I don't want to know anything."

"Gem—"

"Really." My voice was firm. "I don't care. I shouldn't have said anything. It was the martinis talking."

. . .

That night sleep was a slow dog on a long leash. I could have counted sheep; instead I read the introduction to *Walden*. It's about this guy Thoreau turning his back on civilization and going to live in a forest. He makes his own shelter, he finds his own food, he philosophises his hours away, his beard grows south. What was Bev trying to tell me? Thoreau only stuck it out for two years, but my father has spent a fair whack of his adult life making baboon noises in the Tasmanian wilderness, stabbing trout with sharpened sticks, smelling like a Hun.

Once upon the 1980s, Hollywood ingenue Liv Tyler discovered that her true father was not waffly prog-rocker Todd Rundgren but Steve Tyler, the infinitely more dynamic lead singer of Aerosmith. How ripped off was I?

# ARTISTIC DIFFERENCES

# In Defence of Crap Films

Roger "Dodgy" Brick is eighteen going on fourteen, and he can be hard work. When he says he's seen too much, he means movies, not life. (Though he would say the line between the two is blurred.) Dodgy can quote Jake LaMotta's final speech from *Raging Bull* verbatim, but his social skills leave a lot to be desired. He has no problem telling customers exactly what he thinks of their choices. Which is ironic when you consider his secret fondness for crap films. For all his bleating about *auteur theory* and *artistic integrity*, Dodgy is most alive when faced with bad acting, visible boom mikes, wayward dubbing, and fake beards. His official line is that you will never make anything great unless you understand crap. I don't know about *that*, but I do know that crap is contagious. Dodgy's aim to make me a cinéaste has fallen by the wayside. I never dreamed I'd become so acquainted with Eric Roberts's oeuvre (basically his pectorals and arse cheeks).

When I rolled into work on Sunday afternoon, Dodgy greeted me without taking his eyes off the small screen. We had one of our rapid-fire, film noir dialogues.

ME: "What's on?"

DODGY: "Crap."

"Specifically?"

"Jan-Michael Vincent." He pushed a video cover across the counter.

ME: "Remind me?"

DODGY: "*Big Wednesday, The Mechanic.*"

"Why's the sound off?"

"The dialogue."

"Good-bad or bad-bad?"

"Abysmal."

On-screen a guy with a mullet and a face like a bulldog shifted leaves around a swimming pool.

"That's Chris," Dodgy explained. "The houseboy. JMV's hired him to look after his wife. She's sultry but psycho."

Cue the wife, who enters in a high-cut bikini. She has that forgettable page-three-girl look—a would-be star too poorly lit to shine. She opens her mouth and issues an invitation. The houseboy palpitates on the spot.

"Wow." I let out a low, sarcastic whistle. "She's really got something." Dodgy's eyes clicked with mine. We shared smug video clerk smiles.

Dodgy's top five movies are *Rashomon*, *Reservoir Dogs*, *Wild at Heart*, *Le Samouraï*, and pretty much any Scorsese except for that olde worlde cheese that had Michelle Pfeiffer in it. He likes to think he's above the boss, the customer, me—even Marco. Lo says this kind of behaviour suggests that Dodgy has zero self-esteem and is in a world of pain. World of pimples perhaps—Dodgy wears his hormones on his face. The fluorescent shop lights do him no favours, but in the dim-lit stock room it's a different story. Beneath the blemishes, his bone structure is pleasingly symmetrical. Another plus is he's tall, and his hair always looks freshly washed. But then there's his polyester "pachuco" pants, his gross overconfidence. What is it called when you're repelled and attracted to someone at the same time? I mean, is there a word for that?

At Video Nasties we take it in turns to play movies. I was torn between choosing something sexy (to give Dodgy ideas) or something educational (to give me ideas). Then I found a film that had the potential to do both. It was called *Ciao! Manhattan* and it was all about Edie Sedgwick. The back cover showed her with her top off (sexy) while the blurb blared, "*The* Citizen Kane *of the drug generation*" (educational).

Dodgy inched his stool closer. "Good pick."

The film was choppy and experimental. The sound was gluggy and the colour was grainy. Edie was beautiful, but if this film was a true indicator, she'd had a personality bypass. First she was hitchhiking topless. Then she passed out. Then she was lolling in an empty swimming pool, reflecting on her glory days, waiting for royalties or death, whichever came first.

"What a car crash," Dodgy said, shaking his head.

"You don't think she's pretty?"

Dodgy curled his lip. "Pretty vacant."

"I kind of like her," I admitted. "I mean, I like that she's not self-conscious at all."

"That's because she's got no self." This was Dodgy being deep. He had a sore-looking zit in the middle of his forehead—like a third eye. I tried not to stare at it.

"How so?" I asked.

"If you think photographs steal souls, then imagine the power of film. Think about it."

I had a sudden flash of a photo of me and Lo and Mira. It was taken at the height of Satan Summer. We were a rhapsody in black, baring our teeth, giving the camera the devil's salute. I used to get a shivery thrill-full feeling when I looked at the photo. We were high priestesses, bound by words and deeds. But now it occurred to me that I didn't even know where the photo was.

"Andy Warhol filmed everything," I said authoritatively.

Dodgy indicated to the screen. "Hence, car crash." And now his shoulders slumped, and his voice seemed sad. "Edie gave film the best years of her life."

"Maybe it's a good thing. She wouldn't have remembered them otherwise. . . ."

"Ha!" Dodgy's smile looked genuine enough, so I returned it.

"Did you get that loss-of-self stuff from your TAFE course?" I asked him, making a mental note to send off for the brochure.

He shrugged. "Some."

"I'm going to make a film," I boasted.

"You?" Dodgy gave a hearty snort. "How? You got a camera?"

My brave pose wilted. "No . . . not yet."

We watched the rest of the film in silence, but every now and then I caught Dodgy stealing little looks at me— I decided they were looks of surprise and respect and I felt slyly pleased. Could it be that my sudden interest in film-making had given him a sudden interest in me? I thought about all the non-conversations I'd endured with random boys and nearly laughed at the simplicity of it all. I wasn't even *trying*.

The credits rolled. Dodgy was still sneaking peeks, so I turned to him with a cool, "Can I help you?" and then he made me a startling offer.

He said, "I've got a camera you can borrow. If you want."

"Seriously?"

He nodded.

"That'd be great!"

I don't know what came over me. I hugged him—a big clincher. I could feel his chest hard against mine. I could even smell his deodorant—it smelled like grapefruit. I let myself go limp and muttered, "Thanks." Dodgy took his hands off my shoulder blades and put them behind his back. His face was red, red, red. Then his lip curled up as he returned to form.

"Don't get too excited," he said. "It's just video."

"That's cool." I was trying to be just that. "Old school."

We returned to the screen, but it was mercilessly black. All it did was serve our awkward faces straight back at us. To get past the yawp of silence, I started talking. I told Dodgy all about Ug and about the Andy Warhol film at the gallery and how I wanted to write a script but didn't know where to start and I wondered did he have any suggestions and a couple of times I asked him, does this sound stupid? But in fact he seemed really interested, and before I knew it, it was forty minutes past closing time and Dodgy was offering me a lift home.

Dodgy recommended *I Shot Andy Warhol* and *Basquiat* for their biographical content. The only Warhol films we had in stock were *Flesh* and *Trash*. But Dodgy dismissed them as "Andy Warhol presents. . . ." As he drove, Dodgy talked up *Midnight Cowboy*. "You should definitely see it. Schlesinger mixed underground and mainstream techniques. Layers, flashbacks, symbolism . . . There's a party scene that's supposed to be like the Factory. Viva's in it. And Ultra Violet. They're—"

"I know who they are," I said. "They're *Superstars*!"

Dodgy smiled and said, "Right." Then we both shut up for a little while. I was thinking about the video camera. In my mind I was already filming everything I saw: the empty street, the white line to infinity, suicide moths diving into the windshield, the catatonic nod of the dashboard Elvis. Dodgy's driving was smooth and assured. His profile was strong and leading-manly . . .

Outside my house, he cut the engine and studied his hands. He said, "Soooo . . ."

I stiffened. "So what?"

He moved toward me, and I had a sudden panic that he was going to kiss me. I pushed back against my seat. I didn't know where to look, so I looked down.

"Um," I started, "I don't . . ."

He was leaning in. The last thing I saw before closing my eyes was his hand reaching for my waist—or, wait, my breast—or, wait, oh—he was reaching for my door handle. I heard a little grunt of exertion, the telltale catch, and then I felt the warm night flood in to meet me as Dodgy pushed the passenger door open.

"The door sticks," he explained. He had a half-smile on his face that was getting bigger with every passing second.

I was so so glad it was dark, that his car was old and didn't have an interior light to advertise my embarrassment.

"Thanks for the lift." I gathered the videos, my bag, my dignity.

"Hey, when are you working next?" Dodgy asked. His teeth were like tiles. "I'll bring the camera."

But I was out of there quicksticks, marching toward the front door, where Bev's silhouette loomed large behind the lead-light panel.

# *Big Love*

Bev opened the door just in time to see Dodgy reverse out.

"You're late," she observed.

"We had stock-take." I was surprised how easily the lie came to me, and how plausible it sounded. I usually find it difficult to lie to Bev. In the back of my mind I always get the Karmic line: whatever you give you get back threefold. But this was just a white lie, and I had good reason for it. If Bev knew I was crushing on someone, she'd be too much in my corner. I wanted a grace period before she started up with the condom-meets-banana demonstrations.

Bev blinked at Dodgy's headlights. Before she could ask me any more questions, I swanned inside.

"Mmm. What smells so good?" I dumped my swag on

the couch and followed my nose to the kitchen. Bev trailed after.

"Split-pea lentil soup with coconut milk," she announced.

I poked around the sink looking for the soup ladle. Bev found it for me. She took a bowl out of the cupboard and put it on the bench. Music came from the living room.

"Is that Celine Dion?" I asked, incredulous.

"*Titanic*'s on," Bev said. "It started at 9:30. Do we dare?"

I made a face. "Gag." I went to sit at the kitchen table. It was covered in photographs.

"What's all this?"

"Oh." Bev used her arm to sweep clear a place for me. "The Community Centre's having its fifteen-year anniversary. I'm supposed to help make a memory wall."

"Don't go putting any embarrassing photos of me up there."

"You mean like this?" Bev flashed a photo of me as a gap-toothed eight-year-old. I was smiling so hard I looked fit to combust.

I dropped my jaw and my spoon. "Great."

"Relax." She laughed. "It's more for the oldies. Actually, I thought I had some photos from Federation Week . . . maybe they're in the file." She galumphed off down the hall.

I spooned my soup with one hand and sifted through photographs with the other. The Community Centre had seen it all, from book fairs to bingo to ballroom dancing. In the cardboard box on the table Bev had enough "memories" for all four walls, never mind one. I put my hand in for a lucky dip. I was rewarded with a series of snaps of Bev and Sharon looking over-estrogened on one of their wild-women weekends. Underneath these was a small white envelope. Quicker than thinking, I opened it. Inside was a black-and-white photo-booth strip—three poses of Bev and my father. In the first they looked at the camera with mock hostility. In the second they were looking at each other laughing, and in the third they were kissing, her hand on his face, his hand on her breast. Hooley-Dooley!

I put the photo in my back pocket, and picked up my spoon. But I couldn't eat any more. My stomach felt all pinched. When Bev came back out she almost looked like a different person.

"So should we watch *Titanic*?" she asked. She swayed to the music. "I can feel it calling to me."

"Actually, I think I'm going to have an early night."

Bev looked at the clock. "It's only ten-thirty!"

"I know." I shrugged and smiled.

"You're being rather mysterious," Bev said. She gave me her Wise-Old-Woman look, a smile playing on her lips.

"Big study day tomorrow," I told her firmly.

·  ·  ·

I went to the bathroom, locked the door, then took the stolen photo out of my pocket and studied it again. It seemed so private that I felt like a criminal even looking at it. What had they just been doing? What were they about to do? My father looked tanned and handsome, he had a gleam in his eyes, like he knew a magnificent secret. This was the first picture I'd seen of him that made me want to know him, that didn't make him look like a lumpen hippie or a street person. And my mother looked so giddy, so dazed and loved-up. She never looked that way with Don JB. She never looked that way with anyone. This was Big Love.

I looked at myself in the mirror. Was I ever going to feel like that? And then I thought about Dodgy. He'd offered me his camera—was it such a stretch to think his body would be next?

A tingle spread from my shoulders down to my tailbone. I washed my face, cleaned my teeth. When I came back to the living room, Bev had succumbed to the lure of Leo and Kate. I made us both a cup of green tea; then I tucked the *I Ching* under my arm and took myself to bed.

# Inhibited, Needs Encouragment

My bedroom was built into the space under the patio by one of Bev's eco-warrior buddies. Instead of a picture window I have two windshields from a burned-out '79 Sunbird, and instead of having smooth walls to pin my obsessions on, I have burlap over mud brick. But I love my bed. The base is made from railway sleepers, and a beautiful chiffon mosquito net hangs from ceiling to floor. When I sit inside it I feel like I could be anywhere, engulfed in a cloud of possibility.

Outside my window, the moon was bright. I lit candles and Brand Opium joss sticks. I put Bev's Gregorian chant CD on low volume. I found my emergency cigarettes and lit one up. Finally, I sat cross-legged in my cloud and consulted the *I Ching*. This time I had a definite question: "Should I seduce Dodgy?" This was quickly followed by "*How should* I seduce Dodgy?"

My finger fell on hexagram number 35, *Progress*. This was encouraging! I read on. *"Progress like a badger, perseverance brings peril."* My finger wavered on the page. I read the lines again but it was gibberish. Just an inch or so above was the cheerier token, *"Perseverance brings supreme success."* That was more like it. It didn't take long for me to explain away the badger aberration—I was tired, the spicy soup had made me jumpy, causing my finger to slip from its original destination. I decided the "success" line was the true line. I had permission to pursue.

Midnight came and went and I was bright-eyed and bordering on delirium. I was reviewing Dodgy's and my "relationship," looking for romantic clues. He liked to make me blush. Maybe there was something in that. I remembered a night several months back, when he'd cajoled me into watching a schlocky eighties film called *Summer Lovers.*

"Everybody needs a little time away," Dodgy read the blurb in the voice of a sleepy Lothario. "Alone together, no parents, no pressure. One summer they'll never forget."

He stared straight at the screen and asked me casually, in his normal voice, "Ever done a threesome?"

I looked at him side-on, a muscle twitched on his cheek, then the film kicked in. It was set on the Greek island of Santorini. There were hot days on nude beaches and wild nights at Disco Dionysus. Peter Gallagher looked horny, but Daryl Hannah just looked scared.

As if I'd done a threesome! My amorous adventures stacked up to three extended kisses with surplus tongue and a bungled grope.

In chronological order:

1. With a faux skinhead at a party far, far away. He was all teeth. I can't think about him without hearing the theme song from *Jaws* and imagining tonsils swinging like a stiff on the gallows pole.
2. With an anonymous guy last New Year's Eve at the reserve. Me, Lo, and Mira got into the grape. I passed out, and when I came to, Anon's tongue was in my mouth. Maybe the fireworks scared him off because there was a big bang and he was gone. A shower of rosy-cloud rain came down, and I'd never felt so alone.
3. With Mira's second cousin at her parents' anniversary party. Everything about Roberto was short and thick. He kept his hand on my breast but I couldn't feel it through the taffeta. In the reception centre car park he clasped my hand to his crotch. I wasn't sure what to do next so I made a bad joke about cucumbers and that pretty much concluded the evening's entertainment.

Why so few and feeble? I wish I knew. I suspect it's because Bev tried to douse my curiosity by repeatedly telling me how "natural" sex was. Then when I was twelve, I found some adult "literature" at the bus shelter and discovered within its pages a carnival of carnality. I realised there was nothing natural about sex. Call me Daryl Hannah: inhibited, needs encouragement.

. . .

When the credits finally came down over Santorini, I answered Dodgy, but it wasn't really me talking. It was the film version of the blasé vixen I thought he wanted me to be.

"I haven't done a threesome . . . but I wouldn't rule it out."

I was blushing violently. Dodgy looked at me with his eyebrow raised, and I knew I hadn't fooled him.

. . .

Mira says that guys *like* virgins. Lo says the first time is never good. I lay in bed, wondering what Dodgy looked like naked. All my mood enhancers were doing their thing, but I was starting to get anxious. Back in primary school, we used to have to bring in canned food for the poor. No one ever brought anything *nice*, just all the dusty, fusty, out-of-date items from the dead heart of the lazy Susan. Do the poor eat pilchards?

Virgins, I decided, are like the unperishables. If I didn't get a move on, that dust would be all over me.

# Midnight Confessions

"Hurry up, I'm getting bitten to shit."

It was three in the morning and Lo was on my doorstep in jeans and a T-shirt that read "Jesus Loves You." She came in scratching her arms, muttering about the bastard mozzies. She immediately lit up a cigarette.

"Um." I swept the cloud of netting away. "Highly flammable?"

Lo just pointed the glowing ember end at me. "Ashtray?"

I passed her my mug of half-drunk tea and sat down at the end of the bed. "Are you okay?"

"I just felt like getting out." Lo moved over to my mirror and detached the Andy and Edie card. She flipped it over and read Bev's note, "For your project!" Lo put the card back with a small frown. She sat down next to me and smoked and smoked.

"Guess what?" I told her. "Dodgy's going to lend us his video camera."

"Really?" Lo sniffed. "I wonder what he wants."

I could feel myself beginning to blush. I got a glimpse of my face in the mirror. I looked so guy-gone I wanted to smack the side of my head. Instead I changed the subject.

"So how come you needed to get out?" I placed my hands on Lo's shoulders. "Is there friction in the family fold?"

"When isn't there?" Lo rolled her eyes and parroted off one of her parent's churchy slogans. "Apparently, I am 'leaning my ladder against the wrong wall.'"

"Right." I felt sorry for her. "Do they *have* to be so full on?"

Lo shrugged. She looked rueful for a moment and then she brightened. "Actually," she said, "they're away; some aid-training convention. They want to go to Borneo and enlighten the pygmies. Don't laugh, I'm serious. One of the parish overlords is supposed to be minding me but . . ." Lo's smile was covert; not quite nasty, but close. "She's a heavy sleeper."

I had a flash of Lo crushing up sleeping pills and slipping them into her minder's Horlicks.

"Of course," she went on, "the good thing is that now we've got a Factory."

I blinked at her.

"My dad's office? *The New Dawn* is on hiatus while they're away. So I was thinking we could film there."

"But we haven't got a script yet," I said. I felt rushed, tested. Things were moving too quickly.

"Hence my visit," Lo said. "Let's brainstorm."

She hung her head as if in prayer. I mirrored her movements, but I couldn't think of anything script-y. Lo's enthusiasm was grating on me. Did she even know what time it was?

Lo looked up. "Let's do a psychological thriller." She blew out a stream of smoke with the headline, GIRL,17, KILLS PARENTS.

I groaned on the inside.

"Okay," I said. "How does she do it?"

"She uses witchcraft or telekinesis or something."

"More." I waved her on, even though her idea was making my teeth smart. I wanted to say, "Just because it's violent doesn't make it Ug." But Lo was all lit up. She was staring straight ahead, smiling and nodding like there was a big wheel of important thoughts going around her brain.

"Maybe we should start with something less . . . involved," I suggested. "Like screen tests. Andy Warhol used to film his subject's face for three minutes. They weren't allowed to blink or show any attitude."

"Maybe." Now Lo stretched and spoke like a true producer: "I like a film with a cracking story."

"Andy Warhol filmed a guy sleeping for six hours."

"Yawn." Lo exaggerated a slump. "I mean literally yawn. I'm tired." She grinned. "Got something sexy for me to sleep in?"

I went through my drawers and tossed her a tie-dyed slip.

She pulled her T-shirt over her head. I was careful not to stare at the old scars on the tops of her arms. We climbed into bed and let the cloud fall down around us. It was strangely soothing to lie next to someone, to listen to the lullaby of breathing. The darkness made me want to divulge.

"Lo—are you awake?"

"Yeah."

"Dodgy gave me a lift home."

"So what—did he try something?"

"Sort of . . ."

"Gem-Gem, have you been *bad*?"

"Not yet, but soon." I confided, "I think he's the one."

Lo was quiet.

"Lo?"

Now she sounded amused. "This is so slumber party."

"I know." I sighed. Lo giggled and I giggled and we shifted so that our backs were touching. A few minutes later I broke the silence. "I told Dodgy about Ug. He said he'd help with the film."

Lo muttered something.

"What?" I asked.

"I said we don't need his help."

I lay still, not knowing how to respond. Then Lo said, "You're telling everyone about Ug."

"I'm not."

"You told Bev."

"Well . . . yeah," I admitted. I was about to say "Bev's different," but Lo cut in. "What are you gonna do—bring her down to HQ on Tuesday?" She clicked her tongue. "A mother's still a mother."

We fell silent. Time crawled. Outside, the morning birds were starting to twitch. Finally, when my eyelids were hubcap-heavy and I could no longer resist the pull of my pillow, I heard this: "Seriously, Dodgy? He's so bar code. You could do better."

Lo's voice had an edge to it, as if she'd busted me with something far more sinister than having a crush. She almost sounded jealous. I imagined cold rays coming from her body, and I wished she were anywhere other than in my bed.

When I woke up, Lo had gone. For a minute I thought I might have dreamed up her whole visit. But no, there was the cigarette butt in the cup. She'd nicked my boho brown dress with the roses and left behind her Jesus T-shirt. And on the mirror in red lippy she'd written, "Gem 4 Dodgy. Gag."

# Art, Baby

**Film fact: film is a collaborative process—but a vision is hard to share**

If I thought Lo's parent-killer script was bad I hadn't reckoned on Mira's:

"It's a girlfight! I'm in short-shorts and a bra-top and my hair's all braided up like ghetto style. You could do lots of close-ups of my feet, you know, jogging on the spot. Or my boxing gloves pumping the air. Like. So this chick knocks me out, and the crowd storms the ring and it's like mayhem. But then the camera trails over my body and up to my face, and you know I'm okay because I'm smiling, like yeeaaaah."

Mira approximated a stoner's smile for several seconds and then asked us, "What do you think?"

Like, like, like. I looked at Lo and floundered. "I think you've been watching too much cable."

. . .

Tuesday marked day two of study week. I'd spent most of Monday at one with the computer, alternating "serious" study with Ug research. I had square eyes and round shoulders, but I still didn't have a script.

It was a humid morning. Clouds hung low in the sky like a pregnant belly. The senior school was a ghost town. I snaked along the edge of the junior school oval. When I got to HQ, Mira was spreading a red mohair blanket across the cement floor while Lo pulled items out of her bag: a bamboo tray, a bottle of Butterscotch schnapps, three shot glasses, cigarettes, and a silver lighter. We sat cross-legged on the blanket, lit up, and charged our glasses.

"To Ug," Lo toasted.

"Ug," Mira and I echoed.

Lo grinned at me, and I grinned back like she'd never said a bad word about Dodgy or made me feel foolish for confiding in Bev. Maybe stuff said in the dark didn't count.

We slammed our medicine down. My stomach was thrumming like someone had reached inside and stirred it up. I had that grand exclusive feeling again, like we three were the only people who mattered, like everything, *everything* was ours for the taking.

"What's first on the agenda?" I asked.

Lo elbowed Mira and they both started laughing. My grand exclusive feeling began to fray.

"We got you this," Mira said, flinging a scrap of silky material at me. I held it up. It was a bra with gel-filled inserts that made for a bazonkingly bouncy C-cup.

"I call it a boy-catcher," Mira said.

"And I need this . . . why?" I flashed a look at Lo.

"Aren't you working with Dodgy tomorrow?" Mira asked.

"Lo!" I threw the bra at her.

"Sorry. It just slipped out."

"I'll bet."

"This could be the beginning of a beautiful friendship," Mira brayed, batting her eyelashes.

"Shut up. He's not that bad. Not once you get to know him."

"I heard he's only got one ball," Mira said. "Just so you know."

"God!" I spluttered. "Who thinks about balls?"

"He's probably very sensitive about it."

"I'm not going there!" But I was laughing too now. What else could I do? Lo threw the bra back at me, and I put it on over my T-shirt. I looked stacked.

We had another round. Mira and Lo had done zero Ug research.

"You don't care," I huffed.

"Make us care!" they teased me. "Tell us about the Superstars, Gem-Gem!"

So I did.

I told them about Nico, the teutonic blonde who fronted Andy Warhol's "house" band, the Velvet Underground. She looked like an angel and sang like a drone. I had read that she hated being beautiful. She thought it was "so boring" to be pursued all the time. In the Factory days she had a white suit and a black suit and that was all she wore.

And I told them about Brigid Berlin, who was fat and loud and funny. She used to be called Brigid Polk because she would poke a syringe full of speed straight through her jeans. Her parents were society people, and everything she did horrified them.

And I told them about Viva, who studied art at the Sorbonne, and Ultra Violet, who had a thing with Salvador Dali, and Candy Darling, the realest looking man-woman ever. I talked nonstop for half an hour, telling Lo and Mira about all the beautiful freaks, finishing on the image of Edie tickling her throat with a scarlet ibis feather.

"These were women who didn't care!" I summed up.

How cool, not to care.

More schnapps. More cigarettes. I moved on to Happenings. I had come prepared. I took printouts from my bag and arranged them on the blanket like a giant's game of solitaire.

Mira goggled at me. "You're the only person I know who actually spends study week studying. Nerdburgers aside."

"Go on," Lo urged. "Give it to us. I want to hear about mad shit. I keep thinking about how those art terrorists who took the Picasso wussed out. They should have burned it. Or at least drawn another eye on her."

Lo's vehemence put me off-kilter. But I wished I had Dodgy's camera because she was a shot—sitting with her back to the brickwork, next to where some bright spark had written SCHOOL SUX SHIT in Liquid Paper. Lo had her knees up, and the schnapps bottle fixed between her ankles. She swigged from it and waggled her eyebrows at me.

"You can always go further," she baited, but I refused to bite.

"It wasn't just Warhol," I started. "There was a whole movement. There were movements upon movements."

And I was off. . . .

"You've got the surrealists, Dada, and found art; then there's performance art, mixed media, and environments, and that's just the stuff you can classify. Andy Warhol had the Exploding Plastic Inevitable—live music, underground films, and audience participation. All pretty standard—but some of the other Happenings were just mental."

"Like what?" Lo asked. She hugged her knees and thrust her chin forward like a challenge.

"Like one artist put the audience in an empty orchestra pit. Onstage there was a guy being hit repeatedly on the head with a shovel. He had a metal plate in his head, so he couldn't feel a thing, but the audience didn't know that. I think it was an antiwar statement."

Lo lit a cigarette and took short, furious puffs. Mira tugged at the frayed cuffs of her jeans. I couldn't tell if she was even listening. Her forehead was smooth as sea glass. I ploughed on. . . .

"Allan Kaprow—he was the guy who started the Happenings in New York in the sixties—he said it isn't really a Happening unless there are other people involved. But you have to be involved—if you're just watching you're not participating—it's either-or. He did one called *Calling*, where he wrapped people up in silver foil and had them hanging from trees in the countryside, calling out to each other."

I stopped. Mira had dropjaw. I reached over and chucked her under the chin. "Wakey-wakey."

"Talk to me in English," she said.

"It's performance art basically," I explained. "It's performed for someone. There *has* to be an audience. But then you go one step further by actually *involving* the audience."

Lo cut in. "Look, Mira. All you need to know is that at a Happening something has to happen."

"But what's the point?" Mira asked.

"The point—" I started but Lo interrupted me again.

"It's art, baby." Lo snapped her fingers. "It doesn't need one."

I opened my mouth to disagree, but Lo blocked me with her hand. She was a bit drunk and a lot excited. "So when do we shoot? This weekend? Do you like the way I said 'shoot'?"

"Hold on, I've got to do *some* study." I was the voice of reason. "And I haven't done my script yet."

"But we've got mine," Lo said. "And Mira's."

"Yeah, but yours are—"

"What?" Lo gave me the hairy eyeball.

"Shit," I finished.

Was it the schnapps? I don't know what made me say it or even what made me think I had the authority to say it, but once it was said there was no going back. Lo's face went stony. Even Mira's half-smile slipped. The air around us was soupy now, and, like a sign, thunder cracked outside.

"Right," Lo addressed Mira. "We'd better head."

Mira nodded.

"Guys—" I held my hand out.

Lo shook her head. "Don't worry about it, Gem. You study. You've done heaps already."

"Are you sure?"

"Sure, sure," Lo said. But her smile was antiseptic. And as they walked out I felt my stomach lurch. Something had just been dislodged.

# Natural Assets

Wednesday morning I awoke with my virginity weighing me down like concrete knickers. It was time to take action. I had Mira's boy-catcher in my hot little hands and I was thinking why not? I put it on and donned denim flares and Lo's Jesus T-shirt. Then I knotted a flowery fifties scarf around my neck. The full effect was perky and perverse. The finishing touch came courtesy of Inez Wisdom. Her Wicca Love Lotion was supposed to evoke "musk and midnight moons." I rubbed it behind my ears and in the crooks of my elbows, laughed, and did a little dance. Ha-ha! Dodgy wouldn't know what hit him.

. . .

"Very funny," Bev said when I walked into the kitchen.

"What?"

"Jesus loves you?"

I presented a beatific smile. "Jesus loves us all."

"You'll get into trouble wearing that." Bev shook her hands in front of her chest. "And what's all this business?"

"I'm just making the most of my natural assets."

"It's false advertising. The bra *and* the T-shirt. Why don't you wear that nice brown dress?"

"Because I'm wearing this."

"You're pretty dressed up for the library."

"Who said I was going to the library? I'm working today."

"Oh." Bev looked alarmed.

"It's okay," I said, "I'm taking my books. It's not like we get any customers."

Bev sucked her cheeks in.

"What?" I felt a wave of irritation. I was already running late. I'd wanted to slip past. If Bev were a normal parent—that is to say, uninvolved—this would be possible. But no, my mother was a giver. I couldn't leave the house without her offering me something—be it poached pears, French braids, or wisdom nuggets from her worried mind.

"I just hope you're using this time appropriately." Bev sounded more Mum-like than ever before.

"God," I snorted. "Hello, gestapo. You're the one who wanted me to stay up and watch *Titanic* the other night."

"Gem!" She pushed her fringe up with her hand. Her armpit hair bunched out at the sides all grey and grizzly.

"Now I'm late," I huffed. "I was going to ride my bike."

"I'd better drive you." Bev indicated my amplified bosom. "You won't be able to see where you're going." She walked off, shaking her head.

I sat in the shotgun side of Betsy—our 1989 station wagon with the temperamental engine and mismatched doors—and stared down into the deep valley of my cleavage. I told myself that it was okay, I didn't need to be anxious; all I was doing with Dodgy was testing the water. I had to think calm, calm, calm. I was thinking about Lo and Mira too. I'd had a bad night's sleep wondering how deeply I'd offended them. But then I thought about how they were always teasing me, excluding me, giving me shit about Dodgy, about Bev. I had a right to stand up for myself.

Usually Bev listens to the oldies station when she drives. She sings loud and off-key and has been known to toot the horn to emphasise dramatic vocal moments. Today she was a silent promoter of the sidelong look.

Eventually she asked me, "How's your project going?"

"Oh that." I stared out the window. "Okay."

After what Lo had said, I didn't want Bev anywhere near Ug. I'd broken an unwritten rule. It had been a mistake to tell Bev anything.

Bev drove on. I could tell she was stewing. She tried again. "What are you thinking about?"

"That is the *worst* line." I groaned. "No wonder you can't get a boyfriend."

"So what's your excuse?"

"Pardon?"

"If you're the expert, then why are you still flying solo?"

"Who says I am? Maybe I have scores of lovers. Maybe I'm *gay*."

Bev pulled into the service station. "I'm getting the paper," she said. "Tot up your sexual experiences; I expect the sum total when I return." She started walking away and then turned back. "If you want to play the bitch, you should do it to someone who deserves it."

The car in front of us had one of those environmentalist bumper stickers—a picture of the world with "Ignore it and it will go away" written around it. I picked at my cuticles, wondering if the same applied to mothers.

Bev returned with Sharon in tow. "Look who I found!" she trilled. Sharon's overripe bean hovered in the window.

"Hi, Gem! How's study week going?"

Bev answered for me. "In her infinite wisdom, Gem has elected to spend her study week at the video shop."

"Oh?"

"I'm *working*." I glared at Bev. Now Sharon was staring at my T-shirt. "Jesus" in comic font stretched across my rack.

She asked Bev, "Is she wearing that to be ironic?"

Bev sighed. "She hasn't yet learned that you can't go around espousing that which you don't believe."

"Yes, but we all go through that—selective belief. I still catch myself praying sometimes."

"But is it too much to ask for some consistency?"

Welcome to the Bev and Sharon Show, where I'm discussed like I'm not even there.

"This one woke up on the wrong side of the bed this morning," Bev continued. "I ask her a question; she compares me to the Nazis. Were we ever like this?"

Now Sharon was chortling. "Are you kidding—we were worse!" She kept staring at me, nodding, gauging, but she was talking to Bev. "You know what they say . . . creative kids—"

"People." I clapped my hands together. "I'm here."

Bev looked at Sharon and said in her yada-yada-yada voice: "You see what I have to put up with?"

"You're not Jewish, *Mom*," I snapped. "And you're not funny."

Sharon took a step back. "Right. Time to seize the day!" She gave Bev's shoulder a squeeze and drifted off.

Bev got back in and fixed her hands on the steering wheel.

"That was rude."

I shifted in my seat. "*She's* rude."

Bev had been pulling her belt across. Now she let go. It snapped back and clacked against the car door.

"Just how is your godmother rude?"

I shrugged. After several seconds of silence I pointed out, "I'm going to be late."

"We're not going anywhere until you explain yourself."

The car behind us tooted, but Bev ignored it.

I tried. "Why do the two of you always have to discuss me like I'm some kind of exhibit?"

"We don't do that."

"You do." I mimicked Sharon, "*Creative kids* dot dot dot. What's that supposed to mean?"

"You're my daughter." Bev's face had gone bright red. "Of course I'm interested in you." But then I noticed her eyes wandering down to my chest. She started to smile. I was amusing to her. I drummed my feet on the car mat and stared dead ahead. "Yeah, well," I said coldly, "you should get a life."

The car behind us tooted again. This time Bev turned the key.

All along the highway, the blaring radio acted as a buffer between us. I felt bad, knowing that I'd hurt her feelings, that it was so easy to. I sneaked peeks at her. She was acting tough, but she was overdoing it. One hand on the wheel kept Betsy steady while the other floated above the gear stick. She was singing along to the Steve Miller Band about how she too was a smoker, a joker, and a midnight toker. But I wasn't fooled for a second.

# *Existential*

As per usual, Dodgy was staring at the screen when I sashayed through the door. As per usual we went to bat.

Dodgy: "Wagging?"

Me: "School's out. Study Week."

"Nose to the grindstone."

"You know it."

He gave me a cursory glance, his eyes widening at my comic-book norgs. "You look tired," he said.

"Thanks."

"All work and no play . . ."

"I play."

"Huh."

"Sooo . . . what's on?"

"*Two-Lane Blacktop*."

On-screen, two rangy longhairs were inspecting under

the bonnet of a bomby-looking car. The silence screamed in my ears.

"How come no one's saying anything?" I asked.

"It's an existential road movie."

I'd been leaning back against the counter, boy-catcher in effect. Now I curled my shoulders inward. But I needn't have worried. Dodgy was engrossed in the film. I studied his profile. His eyelashes flickered, his nostrils twitched. Every now and then he smiled inwardly. On-screen manly men did masculine things. Time passed. Nothing happened. I was having an existential crisis of my own. I felt ripped off. All that effort and no frisson.

I busied myself nearby, stacking up a pile of returns. Top of the pile was an arthouse film called *Kama Sutra*. The cover showed a naked couple entwined.

"Have you seen this?" I asked Dodgy, flashing the cover. I inhaled and my chest—the inflatable life-jacket—rose up.

Dodgy looked from screen to the cover to me and back to the screen again. "Nope." Then he said, "If you want the real thing, you should check out the top shelf in the stockroom."

"What do you mean?"

"That's where Wal keeps his, ahem, 'adult' movies."

"I didn't know Wal had, ahem, 'adult' movies!"

"Oh yeah." Dodgy gave me a sidelong appraisal. I tried to keep my cool, but a blush was on the rise.

He actually winked at me. "Maybe after lunch."

Down went my head. My temples pounded. My pulse

accelerated. My hypothalamus sent signals to every nerve ending in my body. I was like a lightning field! Surely Dodgy could hear all this activity. I must have stacked and restacked the same pile of videos three times as I searched for an appropriate response to his overture. I wanted something worldly and/or disparaging, but nothing came. So I armed myself with returns, piling the videos high enough to cover my red face, and teetered out onto the shop floor.

"Gem!" Dodgy called out. "I was only joking!"

"I know!" I snapped, a quick save. But I wouldn't look at him. On-screen, Warren Oates's crinkly visage morphed into Dodgy's. He grinned at me and gunned the engine of his custom-built GTO. *Vroom, vroom.*

Playing it cool meant an increase in productivity. After I'd shelved all the returns, I set about reinvigorating the drama section. I rearranged the covers so that my favourite films had pride of place on the top shelf. Looking back over my handiwork, I noticed an abundance of seventies films. Women were an ugly kind of beautiful back then. Or, not ugly exactly, but somehow *ordinary*. Like Jill Clayburgh or Diane Keaton or Debra Winger. I could imagine them in the real world. I could be like them when I grew up. Their apartments had potted palms, copper kitchenware, and clutter. They wore culottes or dungarees with headscarves and turtlenecks. They were independent women with a *social conscience*, and they didn't have to pluck their eyebrows.

When I turned fourteen, Bev gave me a first edition of

Germaine Greer's *Female Eunuch*. It's all about how you should love your body for its differences. Love your third nipple, love your birthmark; your scars are the stories that make you. She was explicit about women's bits. Burn the bra! Damn the douchebag! Don't tame the beaver! Now I looked down at my augmented chest and felt ashamed. I shoved my hands down my top and pulled out the offending pads. I hid them in the case for *ROAR*— starring Tippi Hedren, filmed entirely on location at her mock-African zoo. No one was going to borrow *that* in a hurry.

# The Object of Desire

Dodgy went to lunch, and I thought about studying—for about a second. And then a customer returned *Vertigo*, and I popped it into the VCR and settled back behind the counter. Forty minutes later, Dodgy stumbled through the door with his video camera parked on his nose. I screwed my face up at him, but a smile broke through. He'd remembered! He was making it up to me.

"You know anything about the 'male gaze'?" he asked.

"I know it sounds porny."

"It is . . . kinda." He put the camera down.

"How so?"

Dodgy cleared his throat: "Well, the male gaze is like the eye of the movie camera when it's trained on a woman. It's Freudian. We all sit in the dark cinema and no one can see us staring. And the woman, who is the object of um, desire, plays up to the camera, i.e. *Vertigo* and like you did before; sound familiar?"

"Ergo," I said. "You're saying that the guy's a voyeur and the girl's an exhibitionist."

"Something like that."

"So you're calling me an exhibitionist."

"What? No."

"Good."

I watched Kim Novak disappear into the San Francisco Bay, Jimmy Stewart taking his hat off and diving in after her. That was the problem with desire, I thought. It made you do crazy things.

"Okay, let me at it." I waggled my fingers, and prepared to grab the camera. "How does it work?"

"Point and shoot." Dodgy passed the camera to me. It felt weighty and important in my hands.

"It's so heavy!" I said. "It really is old school."

"*Real* movie cameras are heavy," Dodgy said. "But you're a novice. This will be good practise for you. It'll get you used to thinking filmic-ly for a start. Plus, if you can hold this steady, you can do anything."

I took aim. The camera felt cold against my eye.

"Which button? This button?"

Dodgy fiddled up near my face, a red light flashed in my peripheral vision. I panned around. A customer who had been lingering near the kiddie alcove ducked behind the Wiggles stand. "*Woooohhh.*" I felt giddy. Dodgy was back in view. He looked a little testy.

"You look better on camera," I told him.

He struck a pose. The ice had cracked.

I filmed in a circle again. Suddenly all I could see was black as Dodgy put his hand over the lens. I moved the camera aside and rubbed my shoulder, imagining a groove there.

"Film lesson number one," Dodgy intoned. "No pans, no zooms."

"Why not?"

"These are the first two things that novices do. They get all excited and end up with a film that has no focus. Movies are a series of scenes that have been put in order, okay? Wait—I want to show you something."

Dodgy grabbed the remote control and fast-forwarded *Vertigo*. Scenes I knew well flashed by.

Dodgy pressed play. "Check this out."

Jimmy Stewart moved in to kiss Kim Novak, his dreamgirl. Their kiss went on for ages. The camera circled them, around and around and around in a slow pirouette. Colours danced and spiralled. The world revolved around the lovers.

Dodgy looked proud. He nodded. "Don't even think about doing a long shot, until you've got a reason like this."

. . .

We were both hunched forward, staring at the screen. I remembered the Warhol film from the gallery. Those kisses made me feel alone, but this *Vertigo* kiss made me feel drunk and dreamy. I turned to Dodgy, about to tell him, but his face stopped me. He didn't snort, or smirk, he just lowered his eyelashes and moved in until his lips were touching mine. It wasn't *Vertigo*. I mean, I wasn't swooning or hearing bells or seeing Catherine wheels, but I was definitely feeling something.

Afterward he smiled and said, "Hmmm. Art mirrors life." He cleared his throat and tugged on his shirt collar.

I blushed deep red and stared at the carpet tiles. My eyes strayed over to Dodgy's hands. They had come to rest on his knees like doorstop slices of home-baked bread. They looked like someone had just stuck them on the end of his wrists—he had quite elegant wrists by contrast—without bothering to ensure that all the nerve endings were connected. What if that same someone could lift one up and let it land on my knee?

And then a customer came in and started blathering on about how George Lucas was a genius, and Dodgy starting talking about mythic structure and a book called *The Hero with a Thousand Faces*. I had only one face, and it was gone, gone, gone.

# Progressive Poetry

When I got home, Bev was chopping carrots like a woman who's just had a fight with her boyfriend. I sat on the kitchen stool and swung my legs. Then I took the camera out and started filming. I ignored Dodgy's law and zoomed in on Bev's face. Even out of context she looked harassed and, well, kind of demented. Her eyes were fixed and determined. The skin around her mouth puckered as she chopped.

"What's cooking, Mamacita?"

She paused mid-chop and glared at me.

"That's it, baby!" I did my best Austin Powers impersonation. "That's the look I want!"

Bev flared her nostrils, and puffed her fringe from her eyes.

"Any mail?" This time I pulled an illegal pan shot across the countertop. With my free hand, I sifted through the junk on the bench: old bills, take-away food flyers, receipts, rubber bands, and pen lids. I lingered on the *I Ching* and was about to trot out a random ask when Bev put down her horror-movie knife. She wiped her hands on her jeans and asked in her "reasonable" voice, "Are you going to apologise?"

"For this morning?"

"Yes, for this morning."

"Was I that bad?"

"You can't be rude to me."

Bev willed me to match her stare but I moved the camera on to the mess of carrots on the chopping board. Was she going to make a carrot pesto bake? Yummy. My shoulder was starting to hurt a little. Dodgy said that my new appendage had to be broken in. He showed me the prominent red vein in the corner of his eyelid. An occupational hazard, he said.

I lowered the camera.

"Okay, I'm sorry," I said. "I don't know what came over me. I must be getting my period."

Bev harrumphed. She returned to the frenzied chopping of yore, and I resumed filming. After a while she gave up trying to ignore me and started making little faces for the camera.

"If I were Andy Warhol, you would have failed the screen test," I told her.

"What am I supposed to do?"

"Just look at the camera for three minutes. Only, you're not allowed to blink."

Bev grimaced. "Some other time," she said.

She scraped the carrots into a bowl and started chopping onions. Then she announced, "I've invited Sharon for Christmas lunch."

"What about her Ethiopian extended family?"

"When did you get so disrespectful?"

I delivered my best antisocial shrug. My stomach growled. I started again. "So . . . was there any mail?"

Bev ruffled the papers on the bench and produced a postcard. She thrust it at me. "Just this," she said.

And just like that I felt my energy levels drop.

Rolf. The postcard showed an olde worlde English village in black and white; cob houses with thatched hats. Perhaps he liked the juxtaposition—the quaint images with his progressive poetry on the reverse. I read aloud his latest offering in a smooth and simpatico radio announcer's voice:

> *Dirt under wing*
> *The red-capped plover*
> *Yearns for home*

Usually Bev has a chuckle with me, but this one sounded more like a choke. Her eyes were all misty.

"Onions," she said. But I was onto the catch and gargle in her throat. I read the postcard again, slowly, and this time I took it in. *The red-capped plover yearns for home?* Shit-shit-shit. I was going to have to keep my wits about me.

I cleared some space on the bench and placed the post-card face up with a mock-reverential air. I picked up the camera and zoomed in and out several times. I tried to keep my hand steady but I was all palsied. The shot was going to look like bad tracking.

"Gem?" Bev approached me gently, like I was a wild animal at an open-air zoo. "Gem—could you put the camera down? We should talk about this."

"Talk about what?" I kept filming. I moved backward. Bev stayed where she was.

"I don't know where he thinks home is," I declared. "I've never seen a red-capped plover anywhere near here."

"Honey—" Bev gave me her sad-puppy look, and that was all I needed to crack.

"I've got exams," I wailed.

Bev knew that me crying exams was like her crying menopause. She hugged me—awkwardly over the camera—and let me have a little cry. "I know," she murmured, rubbing my back, "I know, but you could give him a chance. He might surprise you."

"He's a deadbeat dad," I sniffed.

Bev smiled at my childish strop. "He's not a deadbeat dad, chook, he's just . . . he doesn't work well in the real world. He can't live like us."

"Because he's an alien?"

Bev said, "If you met him, you wouldn't think that. I promise. We don't lie to each other, do we?"

Hmmm. I glummed and grunted and hung my head. Bev squeezed my arm. "Don't look so worried."

"Easy for you to say."

But when I looked up, Bev's face was far from worry-free. The lines on her forehead were a hexagram that spelled T-R-O-U-B-L-E.

# Hard to Be a Girl

Dinner was a solemn affair. Bev and I lingered at the kitchen table. After the latest intrusion from my absent father, I figured we were both in need of transporting.

"Do you want to watch a video?"

Bev looked on the verge of reminding me about study again. Then she relaxed. "What have you got?"

"*I Shot Andy Warhol.* You'll like it. It's about a raging feminist revolutionary."

Bev nodded. "Valerie Solanas."

"You know about her?"

Bev displayed her palms. "Honey, you forget. I took Women's Studies under a faculty soaked in second-wave feminism. There were girls in my class who wanted to *be* Valerie Solanas."

"Did you?"

Bev shook her head. "She was too crazy for me."

"How come?"

"She was kind of a fascist. She believed that the male race was a genetic mistake."

"But aren't all femmos man-hating lesbians?" I joked.

Bev frowned. "I hope you know hating the constraints of patriarchal society isn't the same as hating men. Do you want to watch this thing or what?" She cleared the plates and moved into the kitchen. "Put it on, I'll be there in two shakes."

. . .

*I Shot Andy Warhol* was set in 1968, during "the Factory years"—the first mad flush of Warhol's celebrity. The film opened with Valerie Solanas in jail, then her life leading up to the event was shown in flashbacks. Early on, Valerie has a "knee-trembler" with an unsavoury man on a fire escape. The man shoves some dollar bills in her mouth and makes a quick exit. The next shot shows Valerie out on the street hawking her masterwork, the *SCUM Manifesto* (that's the Society for Cutting Up Men.) Valerie's manifesto urged "thrill-seeking females" to overthrow the government and destroy the male race. Converts were thin on the ground.

Valerie Solanas lived on the margins. She definitely had a few roos loose in the top paddock, but the film seemed to be saying that back then craziness was currency—it wasn't as if Andy Warhol was a picture of normality. And yet even in his alternate universe of freaks and subversives, Valerie couldn't get a leg in. She wrote a play called *Up Your Ass* and hounded Andy to produce it. She featured in one of his films called *I, a Man*, but there was no money in any of this. Finally she decided Andy was ripping her off, so she put on some lipstick and went downtown and shot him three times in the chest with a .32. He survived but was never the same again. After the shooting, he closed the Factory doors and upped sticks to a new premises, with a security entrance. Valerie was sent to a mental institution. She's dead now.

Bev and I sipped our green tea. The last song on the soundtrack had minor chords to make us moody.

"I know she was mental," I said. "But I still feel sad for her."

"I read *SCUM* as part of my coursework," Bev revealed. "She had a genius chip in there somewhere; it just got warped."

"I think the Factory people didn't accept her because she wasn't beautiful."

"I think you're right."

"I mean, at least she did something." I was getting a bit worked up. "None of the Superstars wrote a manifesto. All they did was loaf and take drugs and get their mugs in the frame."

"If no one wants you, no one wants you," Bev said, rather mournfully.

"It sucks," I said. I was thinking about Lo and Mira, and even Bliss Dartford, and feeling green. A quick scenario flickered through my mind where I was Valerie Solanas and they were the Superstars and I was trying to impress them and they were being patronising to me and laughing about me behind my back. But then I remembered Dodgy. *He* liked me. Maybe he was a bar code film nerd, but he was still the exception to the rule.

I poured us some more green tea. We left the television on with the sound down. Some bogus reality show was on. A girl only a few years older than me was standing in the shower in her underwear. We watched and winced as she shaved her calves, her thighs, her arms, her armpits. When she turned the razor to her stomach, Bev cried, "Enough!" She switched the television off and looked thoughtful. "It's hard to be a girl," she said, almost to herself. "For every great example you get a dozen bad ones."

I shrugged. Bev stirred her tea. "I'm talking about role models," she clarified.

I didn't say anything; I just let her fall into reverie.

She said, "In third year, the head of faculty was wetting herself because she'd managed to snag Germaine Greer for a speaking engagement—she was on a book tour at the time—but she was a no-show. The faculty was up in arms, and I remember thinking after everything we've come through, we still expect women to be good and polite and do as they're told. Then, a couple of days later, Sharon and I were at the pub. There was a literary function in the next room and who do you think was there? Our Germaine—big as life—she was knocking back beers and tearing strips off a pair of old-boy publishing types. Seeing that was better than any lecture. Sharon said watching Germaine at work made her want to kick in the windows and set fire to the couch."

"Wait—" I said. "Sharon said that?"

"Yep." Bev grinned at the memory. "Once upon a time your godmother and I kicked ass."

Bev's sss's lingered long after she'd gone to bed.

. . .

I was Googling again. Bev's reverie had me all fired up. I wanted to write a script that blasted Lo and Mira's efforts and put me back on top of Ug. I was seeking out heroic women, and guides were coming to me thick and fast: Frida Kahlo had a moustache *and* a monobrow and she was proud of it. And Françoise Sagan wrote a best-selling novel at the age of eighteen and spent her advance on Porsches and gambling. Even Brigitte Bardot, who everyone thought was just eye candy, gave it all away to become an animal rights activist.

I thought about all the formidable women in history who'd made it to the big screen: Joan of Arc, Cleopatra, Delilah, Mary Magdalene, Boadicea, Elizabeth II, Amelia Earhart, Madame Curie, Phoolan Devi, Evita Peron, Mother Teresa, Madonna. They were queens and warriors and whores and saints, and I was going to get Mira to play all of them. Well—maybe not all of them, but enough to show that to be really Ug means you don't give a fig about the status quo. You can be ugly or a virgin or a lesbian, but whatever you are, you revel in it. I logged off the

Internet and opened up a Word document. I titled it THE
F-WORD, and then I started making preliminary notes
toward my masterpiece. My fingers flew like spiders on
the keys.

# The F-Word
# An Underground Concern

**1. INT/DAY:**        **COMMUNITY CENTRE**
    **SCENE 1:**

The Community Centre is hosting a group-therapy session. A GROUP OF WOMEN are seated on fold-up chairs, listening to a female speaker. She has frizzy hair and big sunglasses. She is GERMAINE GREER. Although most of the audience is made up of ORDINARY WOMEN, among them (in full dress) are female icons CLEOPATRA, JOAN OF ARC, MADONNA, PATTY HEARST, KATHARINE HEPBURN, and VALERIE SOLANAS.

**GERMAINE**

For those of you who don't know, my name is Germaine Greer. I am a world famous iconoclast and second-wave feminist. We are gathered here today because we have one thing in common. I'm talking about the F-word. We are formidable women and today we're going to talk about how we got that way. Today we are going to share our stories. Not with shame, but with the pride that befits them. Our stories are vital—especially in this dark age of ignorance. Okay—who wants to be first? (*scans the audience—CLEOPATRA gives her a look*) Cleo? Is that you? Come on up. . . .

Cleopatra glides up in her bejewelled robes to catcalls and clapping. She takes the microphone. Her snake coils around it as she speaks.

**CLOSE-UP** on Cleo's face. She looks proud.

CLEOPATRA
My name is Cleopatra, and I am a formidable woman. (*more clapping from the audience at this confession*)

It all started back in 51 BC . . .

# Be Kind

The birth of my first draft—forty pages!—was swift and painless. I started and finished in the wee hours of Thursday morning, and then spent the rest of the day exploring an online film "community" called moviestalk.net. I downloaded sample scripts and memorised the moviestalk dictionary, which was all codes and capitals letters and things left unsaid between brackets. By the end of the day I knew about jump cuts, stock footage, flashes back and forward, montages with music over, close-ups, crane shots, fades, and dissolves. Movies, I decided, were like life, only better organised.

· · ·

Despite my promise to Marco, there was no Julia Roberts-a-thon on Friday afternoon. Her radiant smile did not light up the small screen. The small screen stayed blank and wanting. I was behind the counter, smoothing my knuckles white and ogling my crush and (maybe) mentor. Dodgy was sitting on the floor, with his back to the file cabinet, and my script in his hands. While he was reading *The F-Word* I was trying to read his face. It was . . . inscrutable. His eyebrows had merged to form a shelf that shadowed the rest of his features. When he finished reading, he slumped to one side, closed his eyes, and covered his face with the script.

"Is it that bad?" I asked.

"Honestly?" His voice came out muffled.

"Be kind," I told him.

Dodgy hauled himself up and grabbed the adjacent stool. He squinted at me and rubbed his jaw. I tried to look composed, but I was arching forward and I'm sure my face was a map of anxiety.

"It's too long," he said. "It's too long and it's too wordy. It's gotta be more than just talking heads."

I nodded. "Okay."

"Film lesson number two: film is a visual medium." He leafed through the pages and then jabbed a finger at the type. "See here, where you've got Cleopatra talking about how she was rolled out of the carpet as a present to Caesar? That's the kind of image we should *see*. Hearing it—boring, seeing it—exciting."

I nodded again. All I could do was nod.

"Something else," he said. "What's the story?"

"It's supposed to be like an AA meeting," I said.

"I get that, but where's your structure?" Dodgy snapped his fingers. "Beginning, middle, end."

"It's experimental," I said, making it up on the spot. "There is no conventional order. The reason you can't *see* is because it's all about the *telling*. How all these stories put together make up one story about the history of formidable women—does that play?"

"Pretty good," Dodgy conceded. He angled his head appealingly and handed the script back to me. I stared at it and understood that 90 percent of it sucked, but instead of feeling depressed, I felt invigorated.

"What if I did flashbacks?" I suggested. "Like, each woman gets one scene that shows something significant. Cleopatra in the carpet, Joan of Arc putting on her man pants . . ."

Dodgy gave me an encouraging smile. "Now you're thinking filmic-ly. Choose your images carefully, Gem," he intoned. "Choose your images like your life depended on it. Film lesson number three: make the film only *you* can make."

"*I* am an auteur," I said, smiling at my self-important tone.

Dodgy looked serious. "We'll see."

.   .   .

The afternoon became "Educating Gem." Dodgy and I decided to realphabetize the entire store. We roamed the aisles, stirring up dust and movie dreams. Dodgy walked me through his personal film history: first film he ever obsessed over: *Jurassic Park*; first film star crush: Heather Graham in *Boogie Nights*; first film epiphany: the backward narrative of *Reservoir Dogs*. After a while it started to feel like I was doing an article on him. I wanted to answer Dodgy's history with my history, but he was so busy orating I couldn't get a word in. As we did the walk-and-talk, I found myself thinking back to our kiss. We hadn't discussed it or referred to it at all. I wondered if he wanted to repeat it. What was our story? Were we just beginning, or were we experimental? Who was directing us?

Right before closing time, Marco appeared. I had been listening patiently to Dodgy's views on auteur theory.

Marco coughed into his hand, "Bullshit!" He reeled on his heel and said, "I hear you're making a film. Do you need actors? I need experience. It can't hurt to live on both sides of the lens."

"Gem's film is *Feminista!*," Dodgy announced, holding up his fist.

"Debase me." Marco clasped his hands together. "I'm dying to be debased."

"Actually, there's no male roles . . ." I stopped and looked at Dodgy. He raised his eyebrows. I held his gaze and then drifted back to Marco, "Have you got a robe and sandals?" I flicked his fuzzy hair, "You can be Julius Caesar."

Marco grinned. "Awesome!"

# Incommunicado

I was comatosing in front of *Neighbours* when Bev came home from work. She rushed off to her bedroom in a flap and came back out, buttoning up her shirt, her jeans almost on.

"Where are you going?" I asked her.

"Community Centre." Bev sucked her stomach in and zipped her jeans up. She whisked a comb through her hair, dabbed on lip balm, and spoke in shorthand. "Memory wall meeting. New Year's Committee. Kevin Dartford . . . specs."

"Specs for what?"

Kevin Dartford was Bliss Dartford's father. Money made him a pillar of the community. He owned a chain of Home Theatre outlets. People called him BD or Boss. His fat-cat vibe was further enhanced by the ever-present stogie fixed between his lips.

"For the fireworks," Bev eventually answered me.

I filled in the gaps: "So you're attending a committee about New Year's at the reserve where Boss Dartford will insist that his fireworks will be the biggest ever, ever, ever. I'm with you."

Bev was pulling tissues and hairpins out of her canvas bag.

"Here's pizza money." She thrust a ten-dollar note at me. "Why don't you invite the girls over—have a study night?"

And she was out the door.

I turned my attention to the telephone.

The parish minder who picked up at Lo's house whispered, "Who is this? Who do you want? Who? Lo? Lo's not here." I hung up and tried Mira. Mira's mother sounded like she'd been at the sherry. "I think she's at the mall, Christmas shopping. Isn't it terrific? They get earlier and earlier every year. I'll get her to ring you, darl."

Nine o'clock came. Then ten, then eleven, then twelve. My cold, cold phone could only mean one thing—Lo and Mira were in cahoots. I sat in my cloud, surrounded by books. I had *Notes from Underground* open on my lap, but I wasn't reading. I was thinking about mathematics. Me, Lo, and Mira. If you tried to draw our friendship, you'd end up with an isosceles triangle: two of us were always equidistant, while the third sat at the far-off tip, which, depending on your viewpoint, could be lofty or lowly. I was used to it being Lo at the top and Mira and I as equal adversaries jostling to get closer to her. But these positions weren't fixed. It occurred to me that I might have the power to bump things along.

It helped to be philosophical, to really believe that it would all balance out. But silence breeds paranoia.

Were they bitching about me now?

Was this a freeze-out?

Lo and Mira were supposed to be my best friends. But it paid to remember what happened to the Rolling Stones. I didn't want to end up like Brian Jones. Kicked out of the band, left to rot in his country home.

. . .

On Saturday night I tried again. I rang Mira, but she was out. So I rang Lo and Mira answered. She sounded all late night and Lauren Bacall, like she'd been swimming in her slip and drinking Chartreuse with the pool boy.

I said, "Miss me?"

She played dumb. "Who is this?"

"Who do you think?"

"Sorry. I've got sunstroke." Mira covered the phone with her hand. I could hear chat, albeit muffled.

"Is that Lo? Can I speak to her?"

Static and squeal, clunk and clatter. Mira came back, sighing.

"She's busy. She said she'll see you tomorrow. She's going over to yours for brunch."

"Brunch? Is she forty?"

There was a horrible long pause. In a film script they'd call it a (beat), or in this case a (long beat).

"I wrote a script," I said, trying to sound offhand.

I heard a clicking noise. Mira's acrylics tapping the plastic.

It was time for shock tactics: "Do you reckon I should let Dodgy do me? We've had one kiss and a definite boner."

I don't know what made me say "boner."

Mira said, "Pass."

My voice picked up a notch. "Can you put Lo on?"

That sigh again, then: "Hold on."

Lo got on the phone, all drunk and shouty. "So the bra did its business? What's the word on the ball factor?"

I snort-laughed. I could hear Lo lighting a cigarette, could see her making faces at Mira while the receiver slipped between her chin and shoulder.

I tried again. "I wrote a script."

"Cool." Came out with a puff of smoke no doubt.

"It's about formidable women. I was thinking about that thing Germaine Greer wrote about the "Great Bitch" and—"

Lo cut me off. "E-mail it to me, and I'll read it to-night."

"What are you guys *doing*?" I hated the way my voice sounded, so mealy-mouthed. I could hear music in the background, bottles clinking, Mira giggling.

"We're imbibing," Lo said theatrically. "We just went to that Clockwork Orange club."

"Without me?"

"You said you were studying."

"You still could have asked."

"Okay, *sorry*. God, don't get weird."

I held my breath. *No*, I wanted to say, *You're the one being weird*. Lo carried on blithely. "Guess who was there—J-Roam and Cola. They crack me up. They want to be in the film. J-Roam said the camera *loves* him."

"I think Bev's calling me," I said. "I've gotta go."

Lo said, "Adios amigo."

The phone went click.

I hung up. I closed my eyes and drifted back to the isosceles. I could see it so clearly: Lo and Mira were twinkling in the stars, and me, I was in the gutter. Who was I kidding? I had no power at all.

# No Blame

On Sunday morning I woke up late, feeling fusty. I lurched up the stairs in my PJs only to be faced with my maniacally active mother. Bev was on the porch in her dungarees, elbow-deep in a pail of plaster. She was dipping stockings in the muck and then draping them around *Magic Man*'s shoulders.

"Hello, Snoozy," she chirped.

"Hello, Busy," I mimicked her. She gave me a sharp look, then went back to her bucket.

She said, "I've given myself a new deadline."

"I've heard that one before."

"The Red Roof Artists are having a show on Australia Day."

"When's that?"

"Reprobate."

Bev pinched the soggy stockings into some kind of shape. She spoke through gritted teeth. "And now I'm giving him bigger shoulders, to symbolize the weight of the world he has to carry."

She squeezed a shoulder; giblets of white goop oozed between her fingers.

"Is he supposed to be Atlas?" I asked. "I thought he was supposed to be Everyman."

"Every man thinks he's Atlas."

"You're a weird beard," I said with a sigh. I leaned against the patio rail and dipped my head backward. The sky was blue and perfect. A few puffy clouds. A wagtail or two. A pair of trainers tossed around a telegraph wire. This was my stock footage. Then I remembered Lo, and a heavy feeling of things being not quite right descended.

"Um, Lo's coming for brunch," I said.

"Excellent." Bev leaned in and bulked up *Magic Man*'s groinal region briskly.

"Excellent," I repeated, watching her work. "Excellent."

Bev slopped another stocking into the pail. She looked so happy being industrious, thick with her art.

"Did you say something?" she asked me.

I pointed to the door. "I'm going to put the coffee on."

· · ·

I was watching the almond croissants defrost when Lo turned up. She looked tired but totally cool in a tuxedo

T-shirt, skinny black jeans, and kung fu slippers. She fiddled with the *I-Ching*, closing her eyes and poking the pages.

"What did you get?" I asked her.

She lifted her index finger. "*Gathering*—how apt." She read on, "Look out: *Heavy lamentations, tidepool of tears.* Oh, cool! *No blame.* As long as it's not my fault."

"It always says that." I took the book out of her hands. Rolf's postcard was inside the cover. I didn't want to get into *that*.

We nicked downstairs for a quick cig, and I showed her the video camera. When she picked it up my fingers tensed.

"Hmm. Primitive." Lo inspected it. "Are you sure it works?"

"Of course. As if Dodgy would give me something dodgy."

At the mention of his name we both made faces. Mine was thrillish. Lo's was like she'd just found dogshit on her shoe. And before I could stop myself, I was gushing, about serious kisses and sexy hands. Lo's face changed from wary-cool to biscuit-blank.

"You actually, seriously *like* him?"

I hunched and cringed and nodded.

"What about all the—" She waved her hands around her cheeks, spelling out Dodgy's skin problems.

"That's just on the surface."

"The one-ball thing?"

"That's just hearsay."

"Oh *please!*" Lo chucked her cigarette in the cup. Its hiss sounded almost sinister. Then she sighed and opened her bag. She pulled out a sheaf of paper. It was my script and it was a mess of red pen—questions, cuts, and comments.

"I made a few notes," she said.

I stared at the pages. "You hate it."

"I don't hate it. I just think it needs work."

"What's wrong with it?"

Lo shook another cigarette out of her packet and lit up. "It smacks of 'school assignment,'" she said. "You know, too much historical stuff."

"These are great women." I sucked my cheeks in. "Their stories make one story." But it was no good. I was trying too hard.

"My care factor on dead women is like, less than zero."

"You sound like Mira."

"And that"—Lo flicked the pages—"sounds like your mother."

I slumped a little farther down the bed. My heels dragged along the carpet. I didn't trust myself to speak.

Lo was putting the script back in her bag. "Leave it with me." Then she saw my face. "What, don't you trust me?"

"Don't be dumb," I said. But the back of my neck was hotting up. And probably my nose was growing.

"So what else is going on?" I struggled to get the conversation back on terra firma. "Have you guys been studying?"

"Hardly. We've been getting the Factory ready. We had a shopping day on Friday. Mira took her dad's Visa card. We bought *acres* of foil."

I didn't like Lo's tone. She was talking down to me, like I was a sucker peer. When I tried to catch her eye, she shook her head so that her fringe fell down like an iron curtain.

# *Blindsided*

All through brunch, Lo made out like she was a New York art dealer and not a bipolar bitch. She ignored me and sucked up to Bev.

She said, "You've made heaps of progress on *Magic Man*."

"I have a new deadline—" Bev started.

I cut over her. "She'll never finish it."

Lo picked at her croissant, smiling up at my mother. I couldn't eat. I felt hateful toward both of them. Why couldn't Bev see how fake Lo was being? Lo and her pillaged wisdom!

Now she was saying, "Henry Moore said the secret of life is to devote yourself to something impossible. Spend every waking hour with it. Give it your *whole self*."

Outside *Magic Man* took up half the patio and obscured the bush view. He was only going to get bigger.

Bev looked chagrined. "Oh, but I hope it's not impossible."

Suddenly a wagtail smacked into the window and dropped to the patio floor. "I wish they wouldn't do that," Bev said.

"That's blindside, not suicide." Lo's face was impassive. "Plate-glass collisions kill over a billion birds a year."

The wagtail fluttered its wings and catapulted itself back into the sky.

"The one that got away." Bev did her Wise Old Woman look. Lo laughed. I stewed over their creepy camaraderie.

"So, Lo," I put on a plummy radio voice. "What's your impossible task? What are you giving your all to?"

Lo looked across at me coldly. Then she turned back to Bev.

"Did Gem tell you about her boyfriend?"

My throat felt constricted. It was swelling up. I kicked Lo under the table. She kicked me back and then she dug me in as deep as possible.

"You know Roger from Videocity?" Her voice dropped to a society hush: "I don't think they've done it yet."

Bev looked straight at me. The blood was draining from my capillaries. "Is that right?" She was asking Lo, but she was looking at me. Her eyebrows darted around. I knew she felt hurt. She was wondering why I hadn't confided in her. I pressed my lips together and studied the wood whorls in the table.

Lo took her knife out of my back and spread some butter on a dinner roll. She said, "You two are lucky. You're so close. I wish—"

Bev drained her glass. "How are your parents, Lo?"

"Pass." Lo got up and took her plate to the sink.

Bev gave me a meaningful nod. I was supposed to go after Lo with a space cleared on my shoulder. Instead I stood up and wavered in my bare feet. "*Whooosh,*" I announced, sweeping my hand across my stomach. "Something's gone straight through me." I repaired to the bathroom.

Ten minutes later I was still in there.

"Are you okay?" Bev called through the door.

I was sitting on the edge of the bath, painting my toenails Lunar Blue. Inside, I thought, No, I'm sick—someone's sticking pins in me. Outside, I hollered, "I'm okay."

Now Lo spoke, her voice clear and friendly. "Gem? I've gotta go. I've got some major cramming to do."

I was thrown. She sounded so normal. I didn't expect an apology with my mother at close range, but I wanted something. Then Lo scratched the door and made a whimpering noise—like the family dog wanting to be let in—in spite of myself I chuckled. She said in a softer voice, "I'll see you at HQ in the a.m., 'kay?"

" 'Kay."

. . .

After Lo left, Bev got started.

"Roger? Suddenly it all makes sense! Why is this the first time I've heard of him? We're not supposed to have secrets."

"He's not a secret. He's just a guy."

"Roger that," Bev cracked, then said seriously, "a guy you like."

My face was burning. "Yeah," I mumbled, "sort of."

"But you haven't slept with him?"

"Mummm!"

Bev's face was crumpled with concern. I knew what was coming next. She put her hand over mine.

"Darling, sex isn't like world movies, all soft focus and sepia tones. Just be careful. Boys your age can be a horror. I should know; I used to sleep with them."

"Tramp!" I joked. I waggled my finger at her. "All of them?"

She looked worried for a moment, like she'd given me ideas.

"I never pictured you with a *Roger*! What a thing to call your child. Like a bank teller or an *accountant*." She shivered.

"He's very nice," I assured her. "And he's very creative. He's the one who lent me the video camera."

"Do I get to meet him?"

"God!" I threw up my hands. "We haven't even had a date yet. You're on a need-to-know basis." I looked at the clock. "Speaking of which . . ."

She'd never been so keen to drive me to work.

# *Trampolining*

There was no time to prep for Dodgy. I had to wear what I had on: old jeans and a hippie top with slippy straps. As soon as Bev was out of view, I foofed my hair, pinched my cheeks, and plucked the sleep from my eyes. My reflection in the shop window surprised me. I looked earthy and experienced—like Raquel Welch in *Six Million Years B.C.*, only not so showy. My hair was wild, my eyes were wary. I felt like I'd emerged fully blown from one of Marco's disaster movies. And I was about to walk straight into another.

Dodgy was leering, holding up some Z-grade filth called *Flesh Detective*. The cover showed a shabby office straight from a forties detective film. But instead of Sam Spade behind the desk, there sat a naked blonde. She had breasts like zeppelins and excessive lip gloss.

"She's hardboiled," Dodgy cracked.

"She has an eighties flick," I returned. "That's so noir.
Is this from Wal's stash?"

"No—this is from my personal collection," Dodgy said.
"I'm kidding." Then he raised his eyebrows. "Want to?"

I hesitated but only briefly. Then I shrugged, my bra
strap pronounced itself, and I heard myself say in an airy,
adult voice, "Why not?"

As he loaded the tape I felt my bravado slide. Mira and
I had watched one of her brother's porn tapes once. We
squealed and laughed the whole way through, like girls
are supposed to. But maybe it wouldn't do to squeal and
laugh with Dodgy.

The film went straight in with the hard stuff. Of
course, I tried to keep a poker face, but all that flesh was
making me nervous. I started to giggle and couldn't stop.
"This is totally gratuitous," I spluttered.

Dodgy held his hands up. "It ain't Scorsese."

"She's not much of a detective," I complained. "And
what's happened to the plot? Where's the dude with the
eye patch? It's messy, very messy."

Several seconds passed with no return. When I looked
at Dodgy he was staring right at me. I swallowed my
laughter like a lump of salt.

"Have I got snot on my face?" I asked him.

"Yeah," he said. "A big globule, right there." He
touched my nose and held my gaze. My shoulder strap
slipped and Dodgy put it back into place. Then he said,
"Did you know there's a ghost in the stock room?"

"Really." I blinked.

"Go and look." His voice was quiet but loaded with challenge.

"All right, I will." I headed off, heart pounding, knowing my jeans were a snug fit, wondering in the back of my mind if he'd follow. He did.

"So where's the ghost?" I hoped my expression was sardonic; though what I was actually feeling was more like scared.

Dodgy came closer. And closer. And closer. Until his body was a chalk line away from mine. "Boo," he said. His breath was warm on my face. "Don't worry," he said. "I put the Back-in-Five sign on the door."

. . .

Video spines stuck into mine as he pressed into me. *This* kiss was hot and wet and it tasted like Doritos. I felt like someone had pressed the fast-forward button down; like we were both rushing toward something, if we kissed hard enough we could obliterate each other. Dodgy had grown many hands. They were everywhere at once. I flashed on a tea towel of Bev's—the one with the multi-dexterous goddess Kali—hands, hands, hands, tea towels. A soundtrack filtered through from the shop: a medley of breathy dialogue, grunts and groans and saxophones. . . . And Dodgy was kissing a trail down my neck.

From the corner of my eye I could see the excess stock assessing me: Nicole Kidman smiling benignly, Bruce Willis smirking, Owen Wilson exposing himself . . . *what?*

I felt fingers rustling my gusset. I thought about tampons. I thought about sea anemones. I moved against his hand like I thought I should, but now part of me was panicking. Questions begat questions: How did we get from *here to here* when just a few days ago we weren't even *there?* When is this going to end? How can it end? Are we going to do it right here in the stockroom in front of Bruce Willis and everybody?

Then we heard the sound of someone bashing a video on the door. I froze. Dodgy groaned, "Fuck!"

My breath was ragged. I sounded asthmatic.

"I'd better go," he said. "It might be Wal."

I did not need a mental image of my boss right then.

Dodgy put all his hands back in place and left. I stayed wedged against the shelf—in between a box marked "Damaged" and a box marked "Anomalies"—and waited for my pulse to return to normal.

. . .

When I walked back into the shop, Marco was perusing the sweets selection. The video player was paused on the flesh detective with her mouth open. Dodgy slipped me a furtive smile. "You all right?"

I nodded, but suddenly all I could see was his zits, and I felt queasy and ashamed. We had added something, and now the chemistry between us had changed. We couldn't go back to being coy with each other.

"Have you heard?" Marco twisted with gossip. "Wal's selling up."

"What?" I squeaked in disbelief.

"It's true. He's bankrupt."

"Oh. Shit." I stared at the floor. Suddenly—mortifyingly—I was crying.

"Oh hey!" Marco rushed over. He hovered with hands like paddles, a nervous Reiki master. Dodgy pitched his stool closer to mine. He rubbed my knee but his hand felt like a clamp. I ran to the bathroom for a cold-water cure. I couldn't work out if I was embarrassed or excited or scared or all three. Mostly I felt sneaky, duplicitous: the one thing I *did* know was that my tears had nothing to do with my imminent unemployment.

After that, Dodgy and Marco acted deliberately "up," playing off each other, trying to make me feel better. They invited me to their TAFE Christmas party.

"There's going to be red wine and Nicholas Ray films," Marco said, "and Dodgy's giving a speech."

"I'm just introducing the films."

"So modest!" Marco eyeballed Dodgy and then he eyeballed me. "When are we going to do *your* film?"

"Soon," I assured him. "After exams. I'm working on my final draft."

"Aah, a perfectionist. I'm going to call you Orson Welles," Marco decided. "*Awesome* Welles."

Dodgy rolled his eyes and jangled his car keys. "We're heading out," he told me, a little apologetically, after we closed. "Me and—" he shone his key chain infrared light on Marco's cheek. "But we could drop you off."

. . .

From the backseat Marco launched into a ramble about Ava Gardner, calling her the doyenne of disaster.

"She was in *Earthquake, On the Beach* . . ."

"That's only two," Dodgy pointed out.

"Methinks she was attracted to these roles because she herself was something of a disaster . . ."

"You're reading too much into it," I said.

"I wouldn't classify *On the Beach* as a disaster film," Dodgy said. "It's apocalyptic."

"Eschatological," Marco corrected him.

My stomach was trampolining. I checked Dodgy out. He was smiling and nodding, smiling and nodding. There was a dimple on his left cheek that I'd never noticed before. Or maybe it was just that I used to think it was a pockmark.

Outside my house I kept it casual. I closed the door and leaned in the open window. My top gaped. I hoped the dusk light would make my sports bra look evocative. "Thanks for the ride," I said. Mira would have winked. I didn't. I was feeling so nervous my body was like wire.

"S'okay." Dodgy pulled up the handbrake. I thought he was going to be gentlemanly and walk me to my door. But no, he idled. He stared at the windshield and idled. Perhaps he was trying to think of something to say.

I was almost at the porch when I heard him call out to me.

I turned.

"I'll call you," he yelled. Then he stamped on the gas and peeled out of there. The last thing I saw was Marco's fist pumping from the back window, his maniac face.

"Awesome Welles!" he thundered. "Awesome Welles!"

# CINEMA VERITE

# The Power Triumvirate

If me and Lo and Mira were fraying in other areas, we were at least united in our cavalier approach toward exams. Or so I thought. I woke up on Monday morning feeling optimistic, almost jaunty, but this feeling soon gave way to trepidation. I hadn't studied nearly enough, and now it was too late. The year eleven finals set the tone for year twelve. A bad performance could send you straight to the arms of summer school. Mira may have moaned about this, but there was no way her parents would enforce it. Bev was a different matter. As I dressed, it occurred to me that these were the first exams Bev hadn't held my hand through. She used to read all my set texts and find creative ways to aid my study. One time she even appliquéd chemistry tables onto the shower curtain. I guess I was a big girl now.

I made my way to HQ for the prerequisite fag and rag,

walking into the block just in time to see the door closing on one of the stalls. Lo stood against it with her arms folded. Her blazer was all wrinkled like she'd slept in it. A giggle floated up above the door.

"Hey," I eyed her warily. "You all boned up for exams?"

She blocked me with a small smile. "So to speak."

I tried to match her tough act. Plucking the cigarette from her fingers, taking a deep drag, and drawling, "What gives?"

"Stand back," Lo warned.

The door burst open and Mira jumped out with her arms up like a stripper in a cake. "Ta-da!"

I looked up. "Bloody hell!"

She'd cut her hair off. Like, *all* of it. What little was left had been dyed baby-chick yellow. It was thick and sticky-uppy like a shag rug.

"Don't you just love it?" She grinned. "Do I look like Edie?"

"You look scary," I told her. "You look like a bootchick."

"Bitch!" Mira poked her tongue out at me.

It was at that point that I saw the flyer stuck on the inside of the toilet door. The letters were cut from different newspaper type and pasted unevenly like a ransom note:

OPEN CALL FOR UNDERGROUND FILM AND RANDOM SUBVERSIVE HAPPENINGS.

# REAR 56 WINTERS WAY.
## FRIDAY DECEMBER 12 8PM

"We're not filming then," I exclaimed. "That's this Friday!"

"Yeah." Lo nodded, eyes wide and serious. "Post our last exam."

"We've put flyers up all over," Mira chimed in. "The book shop, the station, the bus shelter, the brother school . . ."

"So you guys have been busy?" My chest hurt. It felt like someone was squeezing my ribcage. Like any minute now it was going to crack and I'd start leaking. The pain must have been showing on my face, because Lo said, "What's your beef? It's a totally Ug prospect—random and cool—whoever turns up gets to be in the film."

"How does that fit in with my script?"

Lo acted like she didn't hear me.

"We're still using my script, aren't we?" My voice was high and whiny.

Mira cleared her throat and held the corner of her glasses. She sounded like she was quoting: "The transition from page to screen is never smooth. Things that work on the page don't always sound right . . . in dialogue." She looked at Lo. "Right?"

"Word," Lo said. With a straight face.

I stared at them. "Word?" I mimicked her. "Who *are* you?"

Lo shrugged. "Adapt. You think Andy Warhol always had a script?"

Mira asked, "Are you okay, Gem? You look funny."

"I just feel like . . ." I paused. I was hanging on to the outer rim of our friendship, just a hangnail away from falling into the abyss. And the two of them were standing there, so casually, like they'd let me fall and feel nothing.

"I feel like you guys cooked this up and I didn't even get a look in." There. I'd said it.

Blink, blink. They both had witchy eyeliner and Dead Red lipstick on. Now that Mira was sort-of blonde, they could have passed for sisters.

Mira said, "Don't be dumb, Gem. This was all your idea." She looked at Lo, momentarily confused. "Wasn't it?"

Lo nodded. She put her hands on my shoulders. "And it's a ripper."

This was Lo in voodoo healer mode. She could change the atmosphere just by thinking about it—and this was what I loved about her. All it took was a smile, and the right words, and my shoulders would relax. Lo's hands passed pride along like an electric current. I was okay. We were all okay. These were my girls, how could I doubt them? Together we three were a power triumvirate.

Proof came later when nerdburgers Lau Warren and Alita Bean came tearing up the quadrangle, waving one of the flyers.

"Is this you guys?" Lau's face was agitated with excitement. She gripped Alita's wrist. "I told you! I knew it!"

They beamed and nodded. "Count us in."

Lo gave me a look that said, *See?*

I looked at our would-be recruits and felt a twinge of wonder. We were influential! One little flyer had made them break out of years of nerddom. Lau was wearing a crucifix and Alita was sporting a skull ring. They were *trying*.

"What's gonna happen?" They wanted to know.

Mira and I looked to Lo. She just smiled and said, "Crazy shit."

And then Bliss Dartford came up with Paula "Ponyface" Roberts and a selection of nondescript prisses in tow. She also had a flyer. She was pinching it between her fingers, holding it away from her body as if it smelled. She went up to Mira—their mothers still played tennis, so she thought she had a right—and said, "You know about my Christmas party, don't you? Friday night?"

Mira twisted on the spot.

"Read the paper," Lo answered for her. "Mira's otherwise engaged."

"Bliss wasn't talking to you," Ponyface sniffed.

"Hey, Paula," Lo said, "why the long face?"

Mira chewed her lip and stuck her foot out at an odd angle. "We've got a . . . thing on."

Bliss tossed her hair, and said loudly, "Right. Well, everyone *I've* spoken to is coming to *my* 'thing.' "

Then mousy Lau Warren stepped up. "Not everyone."

"Yeah!" Alita Bean challenged.

Bliss put her hand on her throat and coughed delicately. "I'm sorry—do I know you?"

Lau went red and stammered, "You think you're so hot and, and, and you're just *not*."

"Whatever." Bliss bestowed upon us all a tight smile. She put her hand on Mira's shoulder. "If you change your mind . . ."

Lo's face was blank as she watched them walk away. I knew that look: call it the calm before the storm. She said, "Someone ought to bridle that bitch."

There was a dip in the atmosphere. I had the sensation of losing my footing. Lau and Alita looked shocked. Mira giggled nervously. I did not want to be Bliss Dartford.

·   ·   ·

The door to the exam hall flew open, and girls started to file in. As we fell into step I saw Lo ruffle what was left of Mira's hair, "Are we in sync?"

Mira nodded, stout and devout. I clamped one hand on each of their shoulders, and murmured, "What are you two up to?"

Just before we crossed the threshold Lo turned and whispered. "Keep your eye on the time: 9:42."

"Nine forty-two, what?" I hissed back.

"You'll see!"

# Stupid Is as Stupid Does

*Har-ha!*

I was so engrossed in my multiple choice that when I first heard the sound, it didn't really compute. There was seat-shifting here, gasps of recognition there. Then I happened to notice the time. It was coming up to 9:43. I thought the laugh had come from the examiner's table, but the only identifiable items on it were spare pencils and exam booklets. No remote controlled, electronic made-in-Taiwan gizmo that went *Har-ha!*

The second singsongy laugh sprang from a different location. It was louder, closer, and now I recognised it as belonging to Nelson from *The Simpsons*. I scanned the desks for the source—my eyes fell on bonghead Mindy Morello. She looked up, made a face, like, *It wasn't me.*

*Har-ha!*

This one sounded at the other end of the hall, near the plaque that read *Omnia mutantur nos et mutamur in illis* (All things change, and we change with them).

*Har-ha!*

The laugh bounced around. Was it really possible to throw voices? I tried to figure it out. I pictured spy-worthy microphones stuck with wads of chewing gum to the underside of desks, planted into girls' barrettes, laced up in school shoes, fixed into fillings. The examiner stalked the floor with renewed vigour. Sucker peers were sitting up, looking around and laughing.

*Har-ha!*

Lo's face was a mask of calm, her hand moved fluidly over her page. Mira was trying to maintain her composure, but I detected a slight shaking in her shoulders.

*Har-ha!*

School captain Sarah Ferris stood up and snapped to the examiner, "Aren't you going to do something?"

"Sit down!" The examiner looked around the room, exasperated. She stalked back to her desk.

"I'm only going to say this once," she said. "This is no time to be playing silly buggers. Whoever is making that *stupid* noise just understand you are letting yourself and your classmates down and being *extremely selfish*. Stop it immediately!"

*Har-ha!*

The examiner seethed. "You have fifteen minutes remaining."

Thirty-seven heads bent back to their papers. Suddenly it didn't seem so funny.

. . .

Lo finished the exam with five minutes to spare and walked out. Nelson sounded in her wake. When Mira and I got back to HQ, Lo was lying in the grass outside.

"Har-ha!" Mira cracked.

Lo opened her eyes. She was smiling like a shark.

"What was that all about?" I asked.

"Happening number one," Lo said. "Simple but effective."

"And stupid!" I was smiling.

Lo propped herself up on her elbows. "Stupid like one guy hitting another guy on the head with a shovel?"

"I didn't mean that," I said. "Just—they're going to have to grade the exam on a curve now. And Sarah Ferris will probably try and sue."

I shook a cigarette out of Mira's packet and popped it in my mouth. Mira lit it for me and rolled out her impersonation of Forrest Gump. "Stupid is as stupid does. . . ." I couldn't tell if she meant me or Sarah Ferris.

Lo was mulling something over. "Of course happenings are stupid. They come from humans. But happenings also wake us up. They put us in our place. They remind us that we *are* human."

I opened my mouth to argue, then stopped and thought about what she'd said. It made sense. "Nice thesis."

"Thank you."

"So what's next?" I asked.

"All sorts of things," Lo replied, "but you don't need to know. Mira and I have it under control."

"Oh." I frowned. I was just about to ask "But why?" when Lo read my mind. "It's for your own protection. Unlike the rest of us, your record is blemish free. Your record doesn't even have *pores*."

I knew what she meant, but hearing her say it aloud suddenly made me feel as lonely and apprehensive as an exchange student about to walk through the arrival gates.

# Little Happenings

All through exam week the little Happenings kept right
on happening.

On Tuesday during economics, Mira fell backward off
her chair, not once but three times, and each time Lo let
rip the swanee whistle she had tucked in her knee-highs.

Afterward, I praised them: "Very Buster Keaton." But
inside I was thinking, *Still stupid*. I didn't see what Mira
flashing her undies had to do with making people think.
Surely there was a line between art and um, arse? I wondered what Bev would have to say about it. I remembered how outraged she was when that British artist
started putting farm animals in formaldehyde. "He
should live here," she said. "He could build a palace out
of roadkill. There's no difference between that and those
hideous Kangaroo purses they flog to tourists at the Vic
Market."

On Wednesday it was record hot. When the air-conditioner cranked on during the literature exam, a tsunami of duck feathers poured forth from the vents. Several students had sneezing fits. This was better. More poetic. It would have looked great on-camera, but there was no way I could smuggle my third eye into the exam hall. At lunchtime, Lo and I returned to the scene of the crime. I sneakily filmed two year-ten girls sweeping up the mess. They stopped every few minutes to sing into their broom handles. Lo was leaning with one foot against the wall like a New Romantic. "The feathers symbolise flight, escape, new hope," she said, cracking a sarcastic smile for the camera.

Later that day, halfway through cultural studies, Lo took off her red-checked scarf and spread it across her desk. Then she brought roquefort and red grapes from the depths of her tunic pocket and began to have herself a little picnic. The examiner was so stunned she almost forgot to confiscate the contraband.

Thursday afternoon, art history exam: Mira took off her school jumper and kept right on going. Strip poker without the pack. She had on her boy-catcher and a pair of knickers that had frangipannis and the words "Friday, Friday, Friday" printed on them. Typical Mira, primed for the weekend.

That was the one that did it. Outrage ensued. The examiner marched Mira out, and there was definitely something rock-starrish in her pose. Sarah Ferris tried to play deputy, sitting at the examiner's desk, clapping her hands together. "Pens down until she comes back. *Pens down!*"

but no one was listening to her. Everyone was at the window watching Mira giggling and jiggling her way across the quadrangle—straight to the principal's office. Lo shouted, "Give 'em hell, baby! Work it! Work it!"

. . .

After school, all elevenses were rustled up for an emergency assembly where words such as "vandals," "show-offs," and "insurgents" were bandied about. The term Lo particularly liked was "creative hooliganism." The school head looked tired. Sharon-as-wingman shot some pointed looks up the back, where Lo and I were sitting, but that was as far as it went—publicly.

After the assembly she pulled me up.

"Do you know anything about this?"

"Not overly," I hedged.

"Not overly?"

"No."

"Well, which is it?"

"It's nothing to do with me," I said, almost truthfully. Sharon gave me her Look of Grave Concern. "Let's hope so."

On the one hand I felt left out—Lo and Mira were mentally high-fiving each other and I'd been squeezed out—but on the other hand I felt, well, relieved. *It was nothing to do with me*, and I didn't have to lose any sleep over the consequences. Whatever they were.

. . .

As soon as Mira saw me she put her hand in front of her face in classic "no papparazzi" pose. We were back at HQ, and I had the camera primed for our debriefing, but a sharp look from Lo made me put the cap back on the lens.

"So what happened?" I asked Mira. She was fully dressed, but she had panda eyes from her non-tear-proof mascara.

"They gave me a warning."

"Is that all?"

"They're going to review my performance after exams."

Lo sneered. "They're so parochial."

"Mincy was there." Mira dabbed at her eyes. "She kept asking me who else was involved. As if I'd nark. Hey—you should film me doing an open letter to Mincy. Dear Mincy, You suck. And blow."

"Eloquent." I laughed, but I was feeling uneasy.

"We should tail her, film her doing something embarrassing," Lo said.

I didn't like where this was going. "She's just doing her job," I said.

Mira huffed and puffed, and Lo's eyes rolled so far back I wondered if they'd ever return. Then Lo and Mira spoke at once. They said, "You are *so* Mincy's minion," and looked at each other in delight. "Snap!"

## Freak Out

When I got home, Bev was in a weird blue mood. At dinner, she combed her fork through her lentil salad with her face fixed in a frown. When she did speak, her voice was cagey.

"How was it today?"

I shrugged. "Good." I wasn't about to reveal the exam shenanigans. Bev would hear about it soon enough through the godmother telegraph. And I had an important request to put through.

"Ahem," I started. "So, it's my last exam tomorrow, which makes it the unofficial end of the school year."

Bev arched an eyebrow. "Look out."

"And as far as celebrations go, from what I hear it's customary to go out all night."

"Is that right?" Bev was still pushing food around her plate. I hadn't seen her take a bite yet. "Where do 'the kids' go around here?"

"I don't know what *they* do," I said, "but Lo's having a soiree. Just the good people. Thing is, it'll probably run past curfew."

"Will her parents be there?"

"Definitely." I put my head down and ate another forkful of salad. Fortunately the phone rang and saved me from further scrutiny.

I picked up. "Hello?"

A male voice said, "Hello? Hi. Gem?"

It was Dodgy! I blushed and dug my chin into the receiver. "Hi," I said, "hold on." Bev looked up. She had created a continent on her plate.

"I'm going to take this um, out there," I told her, making my way to the patio. "Sorry about that," I said into the phone. There was a yawning silence. Reception was poor outside. The phone clicked and hummed. Dusk was descending, and the parrots were going mad in the palm tree.

"What's that noise?" Dodgy asked. "It sounds like you're in the monkey cage at the zoo."

"It's parrots."

"What?"

"*Parrots!*" I moved back inside, sliding the door shut behind me and sat down on the couch. With one ear I could hear Bev doing the dishes. Dodgy was breathing fast and shallow in the other.

He said, "So, your friend came in tonight and told me about the film shoot."

"Which friend?"

"Mira? The blonde one."

*Ping!* The microwave alarm sounded. Or was that my internal bullshit detector? Dodgy knew Mira, so why was he saying her name with a question mark? "Oh yeah, I was going to tell you . . ." My voice trailed off. I was trying to sound casual, but my heart was thumping hard.

"Do you still want me to come?" he asked.

"Do you still want to come?"

"Yeah!" He paused. "I could swing by after work and pick you up."

"Okay."

"I'll have Marco with me."

"You make him sound like he's a dog!" This wasn't particularly true or clever, but Dodgy laughed heartily, and blurted back, "He is!"

I laughed with him, wondering why our nervousness made everything sound canned. Another great, gawping silence followed, and I wished for a smooth-talking host to cut in and close the conversation for us.

"Okay then," Dodgy said. "I'll see you around quarter past eight?"

"Okay." I was blasé but inside my mind was screaming neon: OKAY!!!

I lay down on the couch and cuddled the phone. Dodgy was coming to visit!

Bev wandered in like a wayward *Neighbours* extra. She was swinging a tea towel and looking thoughtful. She sat on the chair opposite me.

"Who was on the phone?"

"That was Dodgy—Roger." I curled over to face her. "He's picking me up tomorrow night."

Bev's smile didn't make it to her eyes. "Should I make myself scarce?"

"No, it's okay. You can meet him. Just don't hug him, if you can help it." I grimaced. "God. My stomach's gone spastic."

Bev flicked the tea towel on her thigh and sighed.

"What's up with you? Is it the change again?" I joked.

Bev made a little *meep* sound, fast followed by a couple of pregnant gulps. I saw that she'd balled her hands into fists.

"Hey." I reached for her hand and tried to ease the tension: "It's summer, we're supposed to be conserving water."

Bev blinked. "I'm sorry, chook." She sighed again, and then a flood of feelings came out. "You don't know what it's like to raise a child on your own. One day they grow up and they're not yours anymore and they've got their own heads and it's like you never even made a mark. And then they just . . . leave and you're back where you started except now there's nothing inside, just cobwebs and . . . ache and all you are is older and sadder." She laughed suddenly. "God help me, I sound like a Tammy Wynette record."

"You're crazy," I scolded her gently. "You talk about not making a dent and half the time I feel like you're in here." I tapped my temple and ploughed on, "And I'm not going anywhere tonight, so don't . . . freak out."

"I just worry about you." Bev dabbed at her eyes with her smocking sleeve. "I can't help it."

"Let's watch something," I suggested. "I'm so over study. I'm going to look after my old Mum. Let's have a cuppa and watch *Easy Rider*."

"Oh, I like that idea," Bev said, cheering up.

*Easy Rider*, for Bev, is the cinematic equivalent to a pair of comfy slippers and a pack of Tim Tams. Now she relaxed. Her face got a glow on.

She said, "Back in the Paleolithic Age, your father took me to see *Easy Rider*. It was the midnight session at the old Valhalla. It was the middle of winter and the heating pipes had burst. You could see your breath in front of you. Most of the audience walked. But your Dad and I had a blanket, a bottle of cider, and a packet of Peter Stuyvesants. Anyway, I'm not advocating smoking and drinking in public spaces, but that was one of the nicest, most romantic nights we ever had."

I flashed on the photo booth photos and felt certain they were taken that very night. I almost asked her about them but remembered just in time that my father was not a person I cared to know anything about. I gave her my Moonie face, dribbled, "Far out," and flinched for the tea towel.

And so went our Thursday night: my mother and I on the couch, green tea steaming up the ether, and big hippie action on the box. For ninety minutes I forgot about Dodgy and Lo and Mira and when Peter Fonda said, "I'm hip about time," I almost believed him.

# *Machiavelli*

The next morning I almost didn't go to HQ, but then curiosity got the better of me. I arrived to find the block empty. I looked at my watch. It was five minutes to bell. I was just about to leave when I heard swearing and the shuffle of shoes on high grass. I met Lo and Mira out front. They were positively *brimming*.

"Were we meeting today?" I quizzed them.

Lo looked to the left and right. "I don't know, let me check, are we here?" Then she pinched Mira's arm.

"*Ow!*" Mira cried.

"We're here," Lo affirmed. "We must be meeting today."

"I saw your main man last night," Mira teased me.

"I know," I said. "He rang me."

"Oooohh!" Mira shook her head. "He's keen, Gem, he

was *sweating*. What's with those weird-ass pants he wears?"

Lo swung back against the bricks and sang one of Bev's golden oldie Eagles songs, "Desperaaaadooooo . . . why don't you huh hehh hurr ha ha . . . ," and as she sang she rolled her eyes and humped the air lewdly.

"Are you on drugs?" I asked her.

"Wait!" Mira said. "Sniff the air! It smells like freedom!"

Lo stopped humping and smiled. "It *definitely* smells like freedom."

"What have you got for the last hurrah?" I asked. "Let me guess, you're replacing all the pencils with sparklers. At three fifteen the exam hall will light up like a gay disco."

Lo flashed me a noncommittal smile. "Nice—but no."

"No, I really want to know," I said. "It's okay for you, but I want to *pass*. I can't take the anticipation."

"You'll pass," Lo said.

"We all will," Mira droned. She lifted up her skirt to reveal cheat notes written in varying shades of ink above her dimply knees. She stroked her thighs, and spoke like a TV presenter, "Here's one I prepared earlier."

"Show her the rest," Lo urged.

This was some serious tackle: a suspender belt dangling flash cards, a cummerbund of Q & As taped to the underside of her school jumper.

I goggled at her. "You're like a walking textbook."

"It's a cheat suit." Lo looked proud. "You should be filming this." She grabbed Mira's wrist. "This is my favourite." She twisted Mira's watchband over. A quote from Machiavelli wound its way around. I craned my head to read it out: "Before all else, be armed."

Lo beamed. "In exams as in life."

· · ·

There were no interruptions during the English exam. For my final essay, I had to decide who in the current political climate was Machiavelli incarnate. But the world leaders could rest easy. For some reason it was Lo's face that floated through my mind.

# A Good Prospect

Bev had champagne on ice—real champagne—not just sparkling wine. Unfortunately she also had Sharon Minski, School Counselor, cutting up California rolls in the kitchen. As Bev said, "It's not every day my baby aces year eleven. Onward and upward, Gem!" The situation made me tense. Marco and Dodgy were about to front up. I couldn't fathom how high the shit factor would be if they got this close to the elders' gush and gastronomy. And yet, I couldn't be rude. Sharon had even given me an end-of-exams present: a card made by one of her sponsor children and a gift voucher for the Clop Café.

"I've heard about this place," I said. The café-cum-arts-hub on the main drag was where Dodgy's TAFE Christmas party screening thing was happening.

"They're starting a cinema club there." Sharon looked

pleased with herself. "Starting in January with a Wim Wenders retrospective," she added.

"You know all the hot spots," I told her.

. . .

I had the camera, spare tapes, battery, scripts, pens, and paper in a travel bag by the front door. After a dozen outfit changes I settled on a white shift dress with a dusty green shrug, black tights, and workboots. In accordance with *Girlfriend* law, I had highlighted my eyes and left my mouth alone. In accordance with Inez Wisdom law, I had rubbed four different essential oils into my chakras. By seven-thirty I was good to go.

Sharon was on her knees by the stereo. She'd been going through Bev's records, cooing and carrying on, finally plucking out something Afro-Cuban. Now she jiggled on the jute rug, grinning relentlessly. I looked at Bev and whispered, "She's scaring me."

"Shush!" Bev passed me a glass of champers. "Drink this. *Slowly.*"

A squillion bubbles entered my system. I downed my glass and hicced and giggled. When Bev wasn't looking, I sneaked another glass. It was nearly Dodgy-o'clock, and the fizz made my legs feel less plankish. *Mmm*, I thought. *Champagne good.* The doorbell rang, and I saw the scene as if from above. Bev and Sharon had chugged out to the patio. They were watusi-ing around *Magic Man* with their eyes closed and their mouths open. For a second I thought about drawing the curtain on them. But Dodgy and Marco had already let themselves in. Marco saw the elders and beamed. He bobbed up and down to the music. Dodgy gripped the back of the couch. His smile was unconvincing. He looked like his teeth hurt.

"Welcome to my situation comedy," I deadpanned.

Dodgy thrust a bottle at me. "Congratulations."

"More champagne!" I wrestled with the bottle, then spun around and sent the cork into orbit. Bev and Sharon trundled back in at the sound.

"Glasses, Bev!" I shouted. "We're losing fizz!"

I kept the introductions brief. "Bev, Sharon, Dodgy, Marco. Bev's my mother. Sharon's my godmother. Dodgy and Marco are my work associates."

Bev was out of breath from dancing. Her hair was loose; I saw silver strands glinting and wondered when she'd stopped dyeing it.

"Would you gentlemen like a drink?" she asked.

"No thanks," Dodgy replied, "I'm not much of a drinker."

"I'll have one." Marco put his hand up. He raised his glass and then attempted to link arms with me so we could drink like newlyweds. I giggled. The wine was making me grin. With Marco there it was easy to fall into jokey, blokey work mode. I was thinking if this were a buddy movie, Marco would be the loose cannon and Dodgy the straight man—which made him a good prospect: perfect parent-pleasing fodder.

· · ·

Bev had questions for Dodgy. What were his views on pot smoking and driving? What about young men who preyed on drunk girls? When was the last time he'd had his car serviced? What was his star sign?

While Bev and Dodgy chatted, Marco stared at my legs.

"You've got pins!" he said admiringly.

"Shut up." Then I noticed that both Marco and Dodgy had dressed up. Dodgy was wearing neat jeans with his shirt tucked in. Cringe. Marco had an op shop suit on. His shirt was stretched a bit tight, and I noticed some chest hair poking out. I stared confounded at this evidence of manliness. He saw where I was looking. I blushed and quickly pointed to the travel bag. "Can you take that stuff out to the car?"

"Did you charge the battery?"

"Yes, I charged the battery."

Marco hefted the bag over his shoulder and left. I clapped my hands.

"Bev! We've got to go." I looked at Dodgy. "Come on, we're going."

Then Sharon stepped up. She made her sternest school counsellor face, prodded Dodgy in the shoulder, and said, "I want your word that you'll bring Gem home. If she comes with you, she leaves with you. Understand?"

That was some unfortunate phrasing on Sharon's part, but Dodgy handled it. "Of course," he said. Then Bev clasped his hands in her hands, took a deep breath, and went for the hug. She just couldn't help herself.

Dodgy and I walked down the steps to his car. I could feel him dimpling.

"Don't say anything," I said. "Not one word."

. . .

When we reached Lo's, Dodgy popped the boot, and he and Marco started pulling all manner of equipment out.

I peered and poked around. "What is all this stuff?"

Marco held up items and Dodgy identified them for me.

"Lights, cables, batteries, reflectors . . ."

"What's that thing?" I held up a pole that had a bright tubular flag attached to the end of it. "Some kind of party prop?"

"That's a windsock. It keeps the sound in."

Marco interjected, "Actually, we probably don't need that, but it looks cool." He waved the windsock around and made martial arts faces.

I looked past him to Lo's father's office—"the Factory." The building was separate from the main house. It looked like a box on stilts, built high in the trees. The stair rail was lit with fairy lights, and unfamiliar music wafted down from the open windows. I wondered how many people were in there. It seemed pretty low-key for a Happening. On the small platform at the top of the stairs there was just enough room for a fold-up chair and an ashtray. I pictured Lo sitting there, night after night; the city lights twinkling like a promise she could keep.

# Slow Pan

"Gem, what did I tell you about slow pans?" Dodgy chided me.

"Yeah, but I want to get everything in." I had the camera propped on my shoulder; my free hand cupped my elbow. For extra support I was backed up against the wall. The camera was as steady as it could be without a tripod.

"Do it slowly," Dodgy advised me. "No hosepiping."

"What's hosepiping again?"

"You know: weaving, jerking, careening out of control."

"Okay, film nazi. Let me concentrate."

Mostly I had a good feeling from being there with Dodgy. He felt like my partner in film. With the camera between us we could say anything, but as soon as I took the camera away my nervousness would return. If we had a natural progression it was this: embarrassment would pile on top of nervousness and defensiveness would pile on top of embarrassment and pretty soon we were bogged. I wondered how anyone ever got together. And then Marco produced a six-pack, and I had my answer.

. . .

My slow pan started with the scenery. Lo and Mira had transformed the office into a cool, pulsing galaxy. All the walls were silver-foiled. The camera travelled over a shag rug, a dirty divan, some swivel chairs, and an old gramophone. Lo had even incorporated the office equipment. Screensavers of Warhol's Superstars rotated on the monitors. The monster photocopier was sick; its jaws open, its drawers empty. Lo had piled a tangle of telephones on top to form a found sculpture she called *End Communication*. The silver pillows were a touch of class. They were reinflated cask wine bags that drifted across the floor like cosmic tumbleweeds.

I focused on the faces. Our people, the select few, were collected but disconnected. I blamed our absent producer.

Lau Warren's features were small and bunched up like a spitball. She had been earbashing me with her theory about how Lo's dad's parish was actually a hotbed of underground activity, like, one time she and Alita drank so much holy wine they were spewing up stomach lining behind the Sunday school portable. I listened to Lau like I'd skim a school text—taking in every third line—if questions were raised I could still fudge an answer.

Over by the water cooler, Alita Bean looked nervous

and tic-ish. Her eyes winked like Christmas lights. Marco was pitching his latest screenplay—a disaster film set at the Jenolan Caves, called *Excavate!* I let the camera linger on this curious twosome. I'd never seen Marco with a girl who wasn't a customer. He was talking hard, but his eyes kept straying to her cleavage. Alita looked like she was holding her breath. Like, if she kept everything sucked in he might not realise she was fat. Marco wasn't exactly svelte. They could be a roly-poly couple.

Mira was doing the whole lofty, superior femme fatale thing. When I asked her where Lo was, she held her palms up, and I resisted the urge to slap them back to her sides. Now she was at the gramophone, cranking out something old-timey. The singer's voice rolled out like treacle and gave us all gooseflesh. Mira pointed her toes and unravelled her body in a dreamy dance. Her hips undulated; her breasts fought inside her slip dress. She was working her come-hithery glare, but there were only four guys present and they were all occupied. I could tell she was pissed off about the lack of attention. I clucked softly, "Welcome to my world." And I panned on.

J-Roam and his "main man" Cola were under the desk, pulling bongs. Cola kept saying, "Let's bust, homes" and J-Roam would reply, "Word, G"—but they weren't moving. In the spaces between school and home, Cola considered himself to be a Lebanese gangsta. Everything was "bitch this" and "bitch that," but once I'd seen him taking his grandmother to her physio. He held her arm like it was made of china. And J-Roam was a walking morality tale. I found it hard to believe he used to wear tights. The story went that his mother ran a ballet studio. Up until he was fourteen, J-Roam was her star pupil. His talent made him a magnet for bullies. Umpteen toilet dunkings and trouser-dakkings later our boy chose the path of least resistance: hot property, low-grade vandalism, occasional violence. At the start of the year he'd been busted for dealing speed; it turned out to be ground-up antihistamines, but the brother school kicked him out anyway.

My slow pan ended with Dodgy. He was sitting opposite me on the shag with his big, floppy Muppet hands folded in his lap. He said to the camera, "You're going to have hell editing this if you keep filming like that."

"I know," I said. "But now I get this thing like if it's not on camera, it's not happening."

"You're addicted."

"Maybe."

Dodgy cleared his throat. "So, they've got these edit suites at TAFE. I could show you how to work them."

When I opened my mouth, a cheesy American accent came out. "Is that a date?"

I zoomed in on his face. His dimple was in effect, his smile slightly crooked with surprise. He said in a robot's voice: "Affirmative."

· · ·

At nine thirty the door burst open, and Lo's voice boomed over the music, asking the question we all wanted the answer to. "Is this everyone?"

She was wearing black combat pants and an apron top made out of a sari. Her feet were bare. She looked untouchable. She dropped a portable file on the floor, knelt beside it, and started dealing out sheafs of paper.

"Sorry I'm late. Had a fight with a photocopier. Here's the script. Read it and weep, motherfuckers."

The F-Word
An Underground Concern


1. INT/DAY:          COMMUNITY CENTRE
   SCENE 1:
The Community Centre is hosting a group-
therapy session. A GROUP OF WOMEN are seated
in a circle on fold-up chairs. They are female icons CLEOPATRA, JOAN OF ARC, and
DELILAH.


**CLOSE-UP** on Cleo's face. She looks proud.


**CLEOPATRA**
My name is Cleopatra, and I am a formidable
woman who likes to f—
*(the other women clap)*
It all started back in 51 BC, when I first realised how hot my brother was looking. Turns

out he thought I was pretty hot too. Well, one thing led to another, and pretty soon we were—well, let me draw you a picture. . . .

## DISSOLVE INTO CLEOPATRA ACTION FLASHBACK

Caesar is sitting in his easy chair. Two slaves are carrying a big roll of carpet toward him. Caesar's all, "What is this shit? I thought it was the designer's day off," but then the dudes unroll the carpet and who should come out but Cleopatra. She looks hot, and Caesar is madly popping Viagra.

# *Meaningful Glances*

"Oh my God. Oh my God."

Did I say that aloud—or did I just think it? I put my head down and tried not to panic. As I read through Lo's version of my script I had the weirdest feeling: like someone was banging dusters in my head. First came the big bang, then I'd scrabble around the fug, and just when I'd put my senses straight, *bang!* It would happen again.

Dodgy leaned in. "*Nice* changes. *Classy.*"

"I didn't write this," I whispered back. "I mean I wrote that there should be a flashback but not like *that.*" I felt hot—sick-hot. I gripped the script; my fingernails cut little half-moons into the paper.

"Do you want my beer?" Dodgy asked, proffering the can.

I took a huge swig and nearly gagged. Dodgy was onto

page seven. A smile split his face. He said, "You have to keep reading. It just gets better."

**Film fact: The director is always right—unless the producer says otherwise.**

Lo had taken my script about female history, power, and promise and turned it into a farce. But she'd obviously had help—the dialogue was pure Mira: Cleopatra was "hot," Caesar had "man boobs," Marc Antony was "like a total God," Delilah was a "lap-dance queen," Joan of Arc was a "bulldyke." Between them they'd managed to strip my script of all its subtlety, most of its characters, and pretty much all of their wardrobe.

I let the pages fall to the floor and glared at my marauding producer. She was hiding behind her script—occasionally I'd see her brows rise up above the page like silverfish. Sneaky. Meanwhile, Mira was giggling. Lau and Alita were marvelling over Cleopatra's brass. J-Roam and Cola were arguing over who would get to play Samson. Even Marco had folded his pages and said to Lo, "I like it, it's fresh."

Only Dodgy was on my side. He leaned into me and whispered, "You can wrap the chips in that."

Lo shot me a weird look. I made a "scary" face back at her. Her eyes were cool, assessing. She launched into producer mode.

"Okay, given that we don't have a fat roll of carpet, I

suggest we start with the Delilah story. Mira, obviously you *are* Delilah. Lau and Alita, you can be the handmaidens. We need someone to do the lights and music—J-Roam? Cola?" She paused, a smile playing on her lips and then she pointed to Dodgy—"*Hello* Samson."

"Hiya, big boy!" Mira pretended to swoon.

Dodgy blushed and took his beer back. "I don't think so."

"You have to," Lo said. "There's no one else."

"What about me?" Marco cried.

"You can provide refreshments," Lo snapped.

Maybe if she talked fast no one would realise she'd just shafted me. Lo was carefully ignoring all my meaningful glances. I waited for Dodgy to reject his starring role, but now he was rereading Samson's lines. And for someone who wasn't much of a drinker, he was really putting it away.

"Don't let it go to your head," I warned.

"What? It's all fun, isn't it?"

"A-ha-ha-ha," I laughed, loud and desperate.

On the surface it was all fun. Underneath, it was something else. I felt like Lo and Mira were laughing at me. And I felt like they were laughing at Bev too, and all the great women I'd wanted to portray.

Meanwhile, Marco's voice was breaking all over the place as he read the script. "Is she seriously going to be naked?"

Mira said, "She *might!*"

Dodgy suggested, "Modesty patch?"

Lo clapped her hands: "We are not old men. We are not interested in your petty morals." I couldn't believe it! My Rolling Stones theory was coming true. Those were not Lo's words. They belonged to Keith Richards. Courtroom scene, circa 1967. Busted for drugs at his country house. He and Mick got manacled off to Wormwood Scrubs. But where was Brian Jones? Was he even a part of it, or was he dead by then? Was I dead? Lo wouldn't look at me. Mira neither.

"Um, Lo," I said sweetly. "A word?"

She followed me out to the stoop and folded her arms. "Problemo?"

I buttoned up on the Dodgy front and tried to play it professional.

"What happened to my script? You only kept like two lines."

"As your producer I have to say this works better. It's tighter. Everyone is accounted for," Lo said. "And it's funnier."

"You think?"

Lo managed to look bored and offended at the same time.

"I guess you're going for broad comedy," I mused. "Bumpers and headlights for the masses." I was trying to be clever and appeal to her sense of exclusivity, but Lo called my bluff. She sighed, "Don't be precious." Then she tilted her head, "Are you saying you don't want to film it?"

"No, I . . ." I flared my nostrils at her. If I refused to do the film, it was only going to make me look pissy. I would have to swallow my artistic pride and look upon the experience as just that—experience. Lo headed back inside and I steeled myself, Gem Gordon—director for hire.

# Slip into Uncertainty

Lo's interference didn't stop with the script. She wanted to be in on every aspect of the filming. My saving grace was that she didn't know how to use the camera, otherwise I might just as well have handed it over and gone home. More beer had been produced, and we were all imbibing. The drink gave me courage. I may have been slurring, but I was sparring too.

"I want to start with some screen tests," I announced.

"Waste of time," Lo said.

"Actually," Dodgy stepped in, "it'll be good for testing the light."

Lo dismissed him with a growl. "Learn your lines, Samson."

I set a chair up in the corner of the room and had each member of our Happening sit on it and stare at the camera. Each time I tried for the Warholian three minutes, but Lo kept cutting in, tsking, tutting, moving furniture around, trying to put my subjects off. When Alita Bean sat down, Lo said in stage whisper, "I heard the camera makes you put on a *stone*." When Marco was up she cried, "Dude, you look like you've wet yourself!"

At one point I snapped at her, "Shut up!" And she bowed and scraped the floor with her hands. "Yes, Ms. Director. Sorry, Ms. Director."

I was beyond tetchy. It wasn't just that Lo was trying to muscle me, the screen tests showed me something interesting, and I wanted to think about it, play with it. When people first faced the camera, they all started with some kind of pose, but time wore them down, and it was this slip into uncertainty on their faces that I wanted to capture. It made me feel like I was getting something real.

When it came to Lo's turn in front of the camera, she proved she had staying power. I pushed it to three minutes, thirteen seconds until she was the one who went, "Cut." Her chin was thrust forward and her eyes were glittering. And then she said something under her breath. Something short and not at all sweet. Mira heard and quickly looked away. I stood back from the camera, feeling like I'd been punched.

After that I went through the motions. I allowed Lo and Mira to take over placing and prep work. Cola rigged the lights, and J-Roam did some woeful beat-boxing as a soundtrack. Lau Warren was the pancake makeup mixer, and Alita Bean became chief toga designer.

"Is that *Christian* bed linen?" I baited.

Lo ignored me and pulled Dodgy and Mira into her circle.

Dodgy was laughing, liking the attention. "What's my motivation?" he joked.

Lo was droll. "You're Samson, she's Delilah. Look at her. She's hot! She's gonna give you a boner of *biblical proportions*."

Mira smiled sweetly. "And then I'm going to kill you."

Dodgy knocked back his beer and reached for another. He licked his lips and adjusted his toga. I zoomed in on his face. He wore a slick smile, but his eyes were racing. I could see why. Mira *did* look hot. She had stripped to her bra and undies, and her skin was pillow-soft and shining under the halogen lights.

Lo clapped her hands and barked, "Come on people, let's do it!"

I picked up the camera wearily. I wasn't so worried about hosepiping now. The jerking and weaving could only distract from the subpar script. As I filmed I carried Dodgy's line in my mind, "Scorsese it ain't." If I could hold myself above the proceedings, I could just get through them.

# Post-production

"Cut," I hollered. "It's a wrap!"

Cast and crew clapped and cheered, and I leaned against the wall, feeling dazed. I put the camera down. Without it I felt naked—not Mira naked—more like . . . exposed. I couldn't look at Dodgy without feeling hurt. He was having so much fun I hardly recognised him. He'd soldiered through the read-through like he had a gun to his fulsome Samson wig, but by the third take he was delivering his lines with his dimple a'twinkling and his top lip Elvis-ly curling up. Even now, he hadn't moved from the couch. He was pulling his wig over his eyes, making Mira laugh. Lo had her head in a cupboard. She passed Marco bottles of brandy, gin, curaçao, and Kahlua, and he concocted a rocket fuel so potent I should have been able to guess how things would go. He lined up shots and jiggled the tray. "Suck 'em up. This stuff'll take your head off."

Mira was up now, dancing around on a high—shooting out the mood lighting with champagne corks, singing, "The stars, baby, the stars!"

Dodgy came crawling across the floor to lie at my feet.

"*Hic*," he said, and swallowed a burp. "How was I?"

I looked down at him. "You were very convincing."

He looked as thoughtful as a drunk man could. Then he held my shoe in his hand very delicately and proceeded to give it a spit-polish. He looked so cute, I almost forgave him.

According to moviestalk.net, no other workplace boasts the camaraderie you find on a film set. With our hard work behind us, the nine of us lolled on the shag and toyed with the silver pillows. Our people will come to us, Lo had said, and for a sweet, brief moment I decided that she was right. How did she know? Had they been there all along? But then I opened my ears. Something was missing. Like now, post-shoot, there should have been a debriefing, a revelling in favourite scenes. As director, I should have at least had an argument with someone that ended up with either of us saying, "Whatever, I'm not married to it."

My tremor turned into a slow wave of depression. Our people's conversation gave no indication that subversive activity had just occurred. We could have been talking about art and image and the meaning of reality; instead we were talking about Bliss Dartford. Whenever I tried to turn the conversation back to the film ("Hey guys, what about when Mira dances aside and you get the reveal of

Dodgy blue in the face?"), my bleats dissipated like burps. There would be no précis, only gossip. Even Dodgy wasn't listening—he was getting very hands-on. "Are you ticklish?" he whispered. "I'll bet you are." His face was pink from all the drink.

I felt Lo shooting me guarded little looks.

I gave up. The only thing for it was to get shit-faced.

. . .

"I heard from Chrissie Whitelaw that Mindy Morello was seeing some guy from the tech, and she said that he said that Bliss Dartford is like, on high rotation with Pete Wig and that guy with the bull mastiff who hangs outside Nando's. Like, she's doing both of them? Can you believe it?"

I couldn't believe that that was debate team, maths-head, mousy Lau Warren talking. I filmed her face. She was verbose and gross, chewing the words with her mouth open.

Tales of Bliss swirled around the room like vapours. Even Alita broke from her gargling session with Marco to put a few words in.

"Remember year-seven Kris Kringle? Bliss gave me a stapler with a note attached, 'For your stomach.' Bitch!"

"Bitch!" Mira's eyes were huge and laughing.

"Bitch!" Lau pressed her lips together.

"Bitch!" J-Roam mocked them in a high-pitched "lay-dees" voice.

Cola pointed out, "Thass where da party is, hotties wall to wall."

This introduced a new round about Bliss's last Christmas blowout. We three were indisposed, but according to Lau and Alita the party went *off*.

They talked in tandem.

"Maria O'Glia rooted some guy on the front lawn."

"Slag!"

"And the neighbours called the cops!"

"I know!"

"What about that guy who tripped out on Bliss's brother's epilepsy tablets?"

"They found him the next day in the cactus."

"The prickly pear!"

"Guy looked like a voodoo doll."

"She had a keg last year."

"I heard there's going to be two kegs this year."

"*So* teen movie!" They laughed and laughed.

. . .

Amid rumours of a rock band made up of brother school elevens whose lead singer looked like Vince Vaughn, gay jocks, liberated nerds, the inevitable slew of date-rapers with their pockets full of roofies, it came to pass that our little Happening was about to happen elsewhere. Specifically, Bliss Dartford was going to get it. We were going to crash her party.

Lo poured us all final shots, and I started to pack the camera away.

"You'd better bring a spare tape," she said. "Above all else, be armed." I did as I was told. I carried my bag and along with it a sinking feeling that started in my brain and went all the way down to my toes.

# So Teen Movie

Bliss Dartford's house on the hill looked exactly as I remembered it from her fourteenth birthday party. That would be the one where Bliss and Mira made me over with Bliss's mother's Nutrimetics supply to a template provided by *Girlfriend*. Like canny plastic surgeons, they refused to let me see a mirror. Bliss's brother gave it away when he started calling me Priscilla, as in *Priscilla, Queen of the Desert*. I was mortified. I wanted to be transformed—who doesn't at fourteen?—but not into an aging transvestite!

In the Mira-Bliss-Gem triangle of old, I was always on the outer, never on par. Walking up the long drive, just a "hey you guys" behind Lo and Mira, I found myself wondering why I was the one who got practised on and pushed aside when something better came along.

I stopped in the centre of the driveway. Our people

rushed on, heady with hooligan spirit. The bushes rustled and wind knocked the coloured lanterns about. I felt like I was the only thing in the world not moving.

. . .

Inside, the party looked like something out of a John Hughes film. Ixnay on the parental authority figures and bring on the juvenile delinquents! Mindy Morello and the tech boys were shot-gunning beers and spazzing out on the punch; a closed set with that private-school patina were sucking back billies, and couples were dry-humping in the dark recesses. There was a karaoke machine set up on a makeshift stage, and Paula Ponyface was up there, warbling along to Celine Dion or some other menopause music from Bliss's mother's CD collection. A big plasma screen behind her was showing *Video Hits* with the sound down. A handful of drunk girls swayed at her feet while beefy guys threw corn chips at her.

"This is so bourgeois," Lo said, ashing her cigarette on the floor.

Cola boogied into the crowd of slouch-dancing manks, while J-Roam instigated stereo warfare, putting on "somethang for all a y'all bitches and hos." He folded his arms and faced off the naysayers: the *Video Hits* girls, the lurker nerd boys hoping to brush boob under the guise of dance. This was my generation! These were the kids who manned the mall and made baby boomers cling to their central locking. The camera separated me from the action.

I filmed Cola as he bungled backspins on the parquet floor. A crowd failed to gather around him.

One of Bliss's stoolies must have put the word out, because the hostess herself came teetering over, fresh from the spa with some jock's T-shirt clinging to her bikini top.

"You made it!" She brayed in Mira's face. Mira weaved drunkenly. Lo was looking around the room, her forehead creased. She was unimpressed.

Bliss turned to Lo. "Wanted to see how the other half live?"

"Yeah, right," Lo said. "Lifestyles of the rich and gormless."

Bliss's bottom lip dropped. After a beat.

"She's joking," Mira called out as Bliss stomped off. She turned to Lo. "She'll kick us out!"

"She doesn't have the guts," Lo said. "Let's check out upstairs."

·  ·  ·

The walls of Bliss's bedroom were papered in supermodels: the imperious eyes of Kate and Heidi and Shalom and Amber and Gisele were upon us. Lo went for the chest of drawers. Even Bliss's underpants were neatly folded and colour-coordinated. Lo put her hand in and mussed things up. I stopped filming and asked, "Isn't being a neat-freak like a sure sign of something to hide?"

"Eating disorder." Mira was looking through her wardrobe, holding Bliss's skinny-mini dresses up against herself and frowning.

"She hasn't got any books," I noted. "A room with no books is like a person with no soul."

"There's this." Lo held up a notebook with a red velvet cover. She sat cross-legged on the bed and started reading. Her voice was Bliss on helium:

Pony is a loser and a hanger. I know where she gets it from because her mother is *worse*. I saw her playing tennis with mine and Mrs. Roberts was licking up everything my mother said. Pony's exactly the same. And I can't believe she thinks Mark Petrakis would even go there. I mean, hello? Maybe after you get like rhinoplasty and lose a stone and do something with your frizz. . . .

"She really is a bitch!" I marvelled, and my heart went out for Pony.

"I'll have this." Lo tore the page out and put it in her pocket.

Mira thought about it: "She's right, though. I mean it's harsh, but it's true—Pony's pretty ugly. She's got that man face."

"Man face, horseface. She is the queen of Equine," Lo parried. I laughed, but it was just for show. I was thinking about Valerie Solanas and the Curse of the Ugly. If Pony-face were prettier, she wouldn't be copping this disrespect. I stared up at the supermodels. Did Bliss think they were her peers? Or were they what she aspired to? People cling to people for all kinds of reasons.

Lo flipped through the diary. "This is good . . . Boss

Dartford's doing the fireworks for New Year's at the reserve."

I put my hand up. "I knew that."

"What about it?" said Mira.

Lo looked pained. "The Happening. The Exploding Plastic whatsit."

"Inevitable," I supplied. "But what are you suggesting?"

Lo smiled. "Sabotage." She saw my face and shrugged. "Or not."

Mira found a pen. She grabbed the diary and scrawled "Slag" and "Loser" across the pages. She offered it up for Lo's appreciation and then dropped it on the floor. She knew which side her bread was buttered on.

Suddenly Lo slammed both her palms on the bed. She said, "I just had the best idea. Let's go back down and tell everyone about the Happening: New Year's Eve at the reserve. Dress like a Superstar. Imagine if everyone here went there. How huge."

"I thought you only wanted 'our people,' " I said.

Lo sniffed. "Four men and a dog."

"Will people know who the Superstars are?" Mira asked.

Lo shrugged. "If they don't, they'll make it up."

We sat on the bed, swinging our feet. The alcohol glaze was on the wane. Lo pulled a small plastic bag out of her pocket and dangled it, saying like a California surfer girl, " 'Shrooms, dude."

I was feeling uncoordinated enough. But then before

you could say peer-group pressure I was weighing up my options. How much fun would I have if my friends were tripping and I was straight?

"Is it a 'mild' high?" I used a mumsy voice to mask my fear.

"Smooth." Lo nodded. "It's the end of the year and you've worked so hard. And this is *so* Ug."

"Oh," Mira nodded, beaming. "This is *totally* Ug."

The mushrooms were wet and cold. They looked like turds and tasted like dirt. After about ten minutes I said, "I don't feel anything."

"You will." Lo laughed. She was bending down to paint her toenails with Bliss's signature shade, Pearlicious. I noticed fresh cuts in the soft skin on her side. Crisscross. Like the innocuous zigzag stitch we learned in year-eight sewing class, way back before Lo even was.

# A Girl Under the Influence

I filmed for ages. Everything was churning and roiling and shining and thumping. I wanted to know if what I was seeing through the lens was going to be what everyone else saw. I tried to ask Dodgy, but he couldn't get my meaning. He was wasted. He kept saying, "Eye of the beholder, Gem." And I kept answering him, "I know! Oh my *God*!" and I was desperate to document the rolling floor. I was off: seasick, 'shroom-sick. I backed onto a couch and sank gratefully, under siege. Random voices and combating music styles swirled around me. If the air had an aura, then it was cloudy and it stank like dry ice.

Marco came up and we had a weird, stilted conversation. He was talking about editing, repeating what Dodgy had said, he too could get me into the edit suite at TAFE no worries. He pressed something into my hand. It was one of those do-it-yourself business cards. It read "MARCO DIX: DISASTER!" and his phone number.

I tried to tell him it was okay, Dodgy had already offered, but then he gripped my thigh and leaned in and whispered, "I really like you, Gem. You and me, we're the same."

I started laughing at him. I couldn't help it. I laughed so hard it must have looked like a seizure. Marco gave me a tight nod. "Call me when you want to set it up." But as he walked off his face was wobbling a bit.

．　．　．

Later.

"Hey! Wake up." Dodgy was shaking me. "Are you okay? Do you want to go outside?"

"I can't get up." I had passed out and now what? Was this a panic attack? I drummed my chest and took greedy breaths. A thin film of sweat covered my brow.

"Drink this." Dodgy put a plastic cup to my mouth and pushed my head back. Sweet warm liquid trickled in. I swallowed, twice, and then leaned forward and spewed it back up in his lap.

"*Je-sus!*" He stared at the mess on his pants.

"Sorry," I blubbed, and then hurled again, this time getting the floor. When I came back up, Dodgy had gone. But at least I felt better.

Suddenly Lo appeared, rolling her fist in front of her face—the universal gesture for "roll camera."

"Now Gem!" she ordered. "Now!"

I propped myself up and took aim. Mira was coming down the stairs, and she was stark naked. At the last step, she put her hands on her hips and threw her head back, laughing like a starlet. All a-jiggle, she streaked across the room to the plate-glass window that overlooked the deck. She pressed back against the glass. She was *heaving*. She found Dodgy sitting nearby and tried to reprise her lap dance. He went all Quasimodo, so she turned her attentions to Mark Petrakis, the controversial bar code boy of Ponyface's dreams. Bliss and Pony started shrieking.

I filmed the sea of faces—they were shocked, gleeful, confused, concerned, offended, envious. I was glad I had the camera for protection. If I took it away I'd be reeling— Mira was so much wilder than me. How had we ever become friends? She was shaking her breasts in Mark Petrakis's red, happy face. His friends hovered and hooted and hollered. I had a sudden dread about how everything could go wrong. But then I realised that even though Mira was naked, she was no way near vulnerable. I kept filming. Mira stepped off and giggled, covering her mouth with her hand. And then she scarpered back up the stairs.

I felt planted. The camera now sat on my stomach like a tumour. My head was all mixed up. I remember thinking something was wrong: that this was some kind of morality play I was filming. Maybe the point of a Happening was to show that how things looked wasn't necessarily how they were. If that was the case, we were still okay. I thought. Or, I didn't know.

# Nerve Impulses

At 0200 hours, Cola arched his back and pissed a fountain of yellow into the spa. I zoomed in on Bliss standing by with a look of horror. Pony was comforting her, rubbing Bliss's shaking shoulders, making noises about the police.

I imagined Allan Kaprow shaking his head. His Happenings were determined, rehearsed productions, we were just trashing the place. I guessed that Alita and Lau would be upstairs now, raiding the walk-in closets, staggering around in Bliss's mother's heels, and draping themselves in her fox furs; they were probably clipping jewellery from her vanity set and writing "cocksucker" on the mirror in la Dartford's own lippy. But really, who knew?

I felt someone tugging at my shoulder. It was Cola. He

was listing from side to side. Just looking at him made me feel dizzy.

"Yo, G. Lo says check the gazebo, like now. Somethang tasty to film."

These white boys from the outer eastern suburbs had never seen a "gat" or Puerto Rican "ho." Their language came from South Central LA via Hollywood and Snoop Dog. This was becoming acceptable. I didn't even laugh at them anymore.

"She wants me to film?"

"Word."

.   .   .

The gazebo was at the back of the garden. Lo was crouching behind the water feature. She had Dodgy's portable lamp in her hand; it was facedown, blinding the couch grass.

"Are you ready?" she whispered.

"Who's in there?" I whispered back.

I could hear soft noises. Lo rolled her free hand. I raised the camera to my face, pressed record. The red light came on, then Lo turned the lamp around and shone it into the darkness. The light illuminated a couple in a horizontal clinch. I gasped and my mouth stayed open. I was vaguely aware that my knees were sore, that I was pressing my eye into the camera too hard. And something else was pinching me as I travelled from the couple's tangled feet up along their half-clothed bodies. Something like dread. I heard Mira's unmistakable giggle. The guy on top of her looked up into the light. He groaned and winced and blinked. Like a caveman. *Ug-ug.*

. . .

I read somewhere that in the best films, the camera becomes like the eye extended, a means of really *seeing*. The camera is connected to the brain, like any other vital organ, and it operates under the same nerve impulses. I now know this to be true because as soon as I saw Dodgy's face in the glare, the camera shut down.

Dodgy stood frozen with his shirt off and his fly undone, looking like a Levis ad. Mira was swearing, scrabbling around for her clothes. I wasn't going to cry. But if I wasn't going to cry I had to run.

"Gem, wait!" Lo called after me. This only made me move faster.

The backyard was an obstacle course. I pushed past peers, sent beers flying. The spa was now a swill of cigarette butts, Styrofoam cups, and stray bikini tops. Inside there was a lot of couching going on. An older stoner guy was dancing on the stage, naked, holding the windsock over his privates.

I raced up the stairs in search of a phone. I opened one door and found a couple doing God knows what. I opened another and there was Ponyface Roberts, sitting on a bed, bawling her eyes out. She was clutching the page from Bliss's diary.

"Lo Hunter is a bitch," she bleated.

I looked at her long, miserable face and suddenly saw myself.

I put a tentative hand on her shoulder. "Pony—"

"My name's Paula," she said acidly.

"Paula." I sat on the bed next to her, but I couldn't think of anything to say. I looked around the room. It was chintzy. Shabby chic. Dried flowers and mosaic mirrors. On the wall opposite hung a "glamour" photograph of Bliss's mother in hooker lingerie. I snorted. Pony/Paula followed my eyes.

"I know," she said. "Mommie Dearest." A small smile. She didn't look so horsey. She almost looked pretty. And then she was all blurry. And magnified. She seemed to be about an inch away from my face.

"Are you okay?" I heard her ask. "You look kinda pale."

•  •  •

FADE TO BLACK

# Halo of Authenticity

Lo got me home. Home to where Bev was waiting up, worrying thin the belt of her terry-towelling robe even though she'd promised she wouldn't. And it was Lo who explained that we'd decided to go to Bliss Dartford's party and some arsehole had spiked my drink.

"But she's okay," she assured my mother. "She threw up most of it and nothing bad happened."

"Where were you while this drink spiking was going on?" Bev wanted to know. "I trusted you. If you girls can't look after each other, then—"

"Bev, it's okay. Really. I looked after her and she's fine."

"She doesn't look fine. What happened to Roger? He was supposed to bring her home."

"There was a fight." Lo was quick, I had to give her that. "A girl got pushed into the brazier, so Dodgy took her to the emergency room."

"Oh my—"

"Oh yeah, it was full on . . ."

I was sitting on the kitchen stool, whey-faced, hanging my head throughout this exchange. If it had been anyone else, Bev would have been apoplectic, but Lo had magic. Her face was sweet and grave; her voice came out adult, smoothing over the bumps in her story. Every word that departed Lo's mouth came with a halo of authenticity. She managed to sound considerate, sensible, and yet nowhere near uncool.

"I knew he was suss, this guy. He's one of Bliss's boyfriends. He was trying it on with all the girls. Gem wasn't even drinking—we were teasing her about being so straight edge!"

Bev's face showed worry mixed with pride. "Oh Gem, honey. You're too smart for this. When I think of . . ." Her lips closed over unspoken horrors.

"I know, Mum." I was crying now. Lo was eyeing me. I felt her silently saying, *Good one*, but there was nothing calculated in my downpour. I'd almost managed to convince myself that Lo's story was true, that she was my saviour, that I was lucky to have her.

"You're all right." Lo squeezed my knee, a little harder than necessary. I snorted and swallowed back phlegm. Smiled through it. "Yuck!"

Bev hugged me so tightly I couldn't breathe. She whispered fiercely in my ear, "I don't know what I'd do if anything happened to you."

# *Real Things*

When I woke up, Lo was sitting at the foot of my bed, smoking and staring at me. Bela Lugosi couldn't have creeped me out more. I jerked upright and tried to talk normally. My voice was anything but. Out of my mouth came sloppy vowels, every syllable set in aspic.

"How long have I been asleep?"

"Four hours. Do you want a fag?"

"I couldn't . . . my head."

Lo climbed up next to me. She started to stroke my hair. "Poor Gem-Gem, you got a hangover?"

I shook my head away from her hand. The drama of the night came rushing back. I had little flashes, like jump cuts: Lo's snakiness, Mira's strip, and Dodgy as Samson, drunk, smiling, posing for the camera.

"Where's Mira?" I had to force myself to say her name.

"I left her at the party."

"With Dodgy."

"I guess." Lo took a deep drag on her cigarette and blew a smoke ring. She shook her head. "I'm sorry you had to see it like that, but you wouldn't have believed me otherwise."

"You could have just *told* me," I managed to say. "But I guess that would have had less impact." I couldn't untwist my face.

Lo reeled back. "You think I wanted to hurt you? Why would I want to hurt you?"

"I don't know. Because you're a bitch? You both are."

Lo was quiet for a minute. I hung my head in my hands and did the full sulk. Then Lo put her arm around my slumped shoulders and hefted me so that I was sitting up straight and facing the mirror. I looked like a sad little goth girl. Who was going to love me? My skin was ashy. The eye makeup I had so carefully applied had gone south. Lo's eyes stayed on mine. I was watching her smile curl up, the arrogant tilt of her head. She had all the answers, before I even knew the questions.

"There's nothing special about Dodgy. He's just a guy. A guy with one ball who can't hold his drink." She narrowed her eyes. "Here's what you should do: Get him to come to our New Year's Happening and then mess with his head. Get with Marco in front of him. See how he likes that."

My head was pounding. I made a cave with the doona cover and dug myself in, muttering, "I don't want to talk about it anymore."

"Let's talk about something else then." Lo poked me through the doona cover. "The Exploding Plastic whatsit is going to go *off*! Maybe we could fuck with the power. Remember that Happening you told us about—the one where everyone was led into a dark room and then terrorised by a lawnmower? Something like that would be cool."

Lo stood up, and as she did her top shifted and I saw again the crisscross cuts in her skin. Even dragons have their vulnerable spots.

Emboldened, I told her, "Yoko Ono had a Happening called *Cut Piece*. She sat on an empty stage and invited people to cut her clothes off." I mimed a pair of scissors cutting and raised my eyebrows at her.

Lo half-laughed. "What a weirdo." Then her eyes flickered. "Do you want to hear my ideas or not?"

*Not*, I thought. I didn't say anything.

She started pacing, drumming her fists on her thighs—it might have been comical except I knew she wasn't faking it. Her face was compressed with possibility and excitement: she talked about sirens, air raids, and teargas; she talked about Waco and airplanes falling from the sky; she talked about kids with weapons, plushies bearing paintball guns, pornographic postcards, hedgeburners, pig's blood, and random punch-ups. On and on and on and on. Maybe she was an android with mangled wires. She was short-circuiting right in front of me. That would explain so much.

She smacked her fists together. "I want to do something

that makes people sit up and *freak the fuck out*! I want to take their *heads off*!"

Maybe I should have been scared, but mostly I just felt tired. Lo's words made a wall that pressed against my brain. She was staring at me now like I was supposed to say something, so I did.

"Fuck the Happening."

Lo laughed, and then it dawned on her that I wasn't joking. She looked mystified. "But what about Ug? The Happening's the whole point."

I shrugged. "I don't want to do it anymore."

Silence fell. Then I shocked the both of us by asking, "Lo, why are you cutting yourself? I know you still do it. I can *see*." I reached for her top, wanting to expose her, but she jumped back. Lo's face changed from peach to pink to crisping crimson—and it reminded me of mood rings, how for six months it was like wearing a rainbow on your finger but eventually the stone would go black and stay that way.

Lo's face had settled on grey. She walked over to the mirror, squatted in front of it, licked her finger, and traced a line along the glass.

"Why are you acting so mental? Talk to me," I pleaded. "You never talk to me about real things."

But Lo wouldn't even look at me. She leaned back on her elbows and raised her foot, teasing.

"Lo!"

She smirked. Then she karate-kicked the mirror. Hard. It cracked, of course, and I saw everything in its sharp jagged pieces—truth, lies, and all the muck in between. The night was over and I was left with the facts: Dodgy was an arsehole, Mira was a bitch, Lo had lost the plot.

Lo picked up her bag. "There *is* going to be a Happening. With or without you."

She left a few drops of blood and a burning fag end. That was all.

# Chunks of Sky

On Sunday I took a mental health day. I rang Wal and told him I couldn't come in due to "personal issues." As I hung up, a mini-movie unreeled in my mind: Wal passes the information on to Dodgy. Dodgy feels bad and guilty and worried for me. He comes around with carnations and Billy Wilder videos. He says something like, "Gem, I was crazy. It was the beer and the champagne and the punch and the rocket fuel. Will you ever, ever forgive me?" And I take the carnations, and I take the Billy Wilder videos, and I close the door in his zit-city face.

· · ·

I was still hungover and depressed. So I commandeered the couch and watched a fluffy fifties film called *Three Coins in the Fountain*. It was about three American secretaries working in Rome. They wished for love at the Trevi Fountain, and after a few hiccups, they all got something like it. I remembered reading an article about the director, Jean Negulesco, that called him the king of the three-girls plot. He said scripts like that just wrote themselves. Each girl was seeking something—romance or a career—and generally what happened was that one girl got lucky, one ended up pretty much where she started, and the last got lost. Which got me thinking, if they made a movie about me and Lo and Mira, who would get what?

. . .

Right before dinner I got the duty call from Mira. I carried the phone out to the patio and steeled myself under the brooding gaze of *Magic Man*.

"Sorry." Her voice was husky and not quite sincere. "I was 'shrooming. It didn't mean anything. I don't even like him."

I wanted to act cool and brush it off, but Mira's betrayal had made a mute out of me. After a few beats of silence, she huffed down the line.

"Hello? This is what happens at parties." Her mouth would be slack now, her eyes rolled skyward. She really didn't get it.

I started slowly. "I know this is what happens at parties, but it wasn't supposed to happen to me. You're supposed to be my friend."

I heard her suck her breath back—she was thinking,

that was something—but when she spoke, her voice was casual-cruel. "Is this about the virginity thing? Um, move on? I mean care much?"

"Mira—"

"Don't be, like, a hypocrite, I was only doing what you wanted to do."

"That's what I mean!" I cried, my temples locked in frustration. "Friends don't do that to friends."

"But it was *nothing*!"

I said, "Mira—let me explain something to you. Dodgy and I were working up to a *moment*. It's not the same as sex. It's more than that, so you probably don't know what I'm talking about."

"Well maybe you should have told *him* that."

Ouch.

"You make me sick!" I snapped.

"Go throw."

I took a deep breath. "You're a bitch. Don't call me anymore. If you see me on the street, cross the road."

Mira sighed. "Gem, don't be an arsehole. Anyway, you should be mad at Lo, not me. It was her idea."

"Yeah right." I paused, straining for the perfect insult. I wanted something stunning that would leave her wrecked and babbling.

Mira made a sucking noise. "Okay, I'm going to hang up," she said.

I slammed the phone down, beating her to it.

. . .

I sat and watched the parrots plunder the cabbage tree palm until it was time to go in for dinner. The sky was changing, getting darker and darker, and a chill was in the air. Bev had made nachos—usually my favourite—but nary a corn chip passed my lips. I couldn't open my mouth. All I needed was a "What's up, chook?" and it would all come out, my own personal tidal wave: I'm still a virgin! My friends betrayed me! I am humiliated! But I knew my mother's rhetoric: never let a guy get the better of you; don't look for a man to complete you, look for a man to complement you; women need men like fish need bicycles; do you think Germaine Greer would be acting like this? A true feminist would never let love get to her. Our Germaine would just face the cad, shake out her hair, stretch her long legs, and say something devastating that would make him regret, regret, regret.

. . .

Bev didn't ask me anything over dinner. She gave me the odd furtive glance and chewed her food quietly. And not much was made of the postcard either. She passed my father's latest missive like she was passing the salt.

> *Christmas, Christmas*
> *All roads converge*
> *To make a new direction*

I read aloud, then let go of the card with a gagging noise.
"He's like the Unabomber. Only instead of getting the

job done in one fat post pack he's killing us slowly with haikus."

Bev just gave me a weary smile and pushed the fruit salad bowl in front of me. "Come on, help me finish this off."

Outside it had started raining—little drops of water, big chunks of sky.

# NEW DIRECTIONS

# *Hypothetical*

My post-party plan was to keep my head down. Thank God for the stealthy approach of Christmas, for shopping and other distractions: Bev's relentless search for the perfect nut roast, my increasingly implausible wish list (a video camera, a new wardrobe, a round-the-world air ticket). I was ripe for reinvention. I wanted to be a new face in a foreign place with funny, sit-com friends and no feelings. Andy Warhol once said he was in love with plastic. So durable, so full of potential, everything just sliding off the surface. I could definitely see the appeal.

I cleaned out my room and did a clothes cull, sorting out a pile for the Salvation Army and a pile for adaptation. I did the weeding, staked the tomato plants, and made a killer salad using red peppers, string beans, and basil from the garden. I even sat down with Bev and the Melbourne University course book. Bev circled Women's Studies, I circled Cinema Studies, and it all felt very hypothetical. And so it went, the days were hot, the sky was blue, the air didn't move. We were having our own Happening, Bev and I. We were less a household than an installation: *Girl and Hippie Mother—Downtime*. I was enjoying it. As long as we were contained, I didn't have to think about anything. I was moving like something in a dream, or under glass.

It couldn't last.

. . .

Saturday marked a week and a day since the party. School was officially out, and I was officially a loner. There had been long solitary walks, just me and Dodgy's video camera, communing with nature. I could spend hours ankle-deep in the creek filming the dragonflies as they whizzed by. I was just returning from one such sortie when Bev called out to me from the patio.

"Gem—where's the *I Ching*?"

"It's in my room. I'll get it."

I found the book and brought it upstairs. Bev had been working on *Magic Man*'s face for most of the day. He now had eyes, a nose, and a mouth. He also had a monobrow.

"What do you think?" she asked me.

"He looks stern," I told her. Actually he looked kind of creepy. It was the monobrow. I tried to think of a nice way to put it.

"He looks like he wants to tell me off," I said.

Bev smiled. "I think you're projecting." She wiped her hands and ventured, "So I thought we could do a reading, see what the next few weeks are going to bring." Something in my stance must have bugged her because she suddenly gave up all pretence of hinting and blurted out, "Gem, I want to talk to you about your father. He's coming, you know. You can't stonewall him."

"He stonewalled me."

"He didn't. He—" Bev took my hand and marched me inside. She planted me on the couch and sat down next to me. I stared at our hands. Underneath the flecks of goop Bev's nails were soft pink like the inside of a shell. I'd painted mine Hiroshima Sunset, and even from this short distance they looked diseased.

She said, "Honey, some people just don't work well in the world. It doesn't matter how hard they try, it's like they're allergic."

I clapped a hand to my head. "That's where I get it from!"

"Gem, listen to me. Your father had problems when he was young."

"I know, I know, it was his artistic temperament." I rolled my eyes.

Bev held my hand tighter. She pushed against it and made a growl of frustration, and then she said, "I made it sound romantic."

"Pukey."

"Gem!"

I shrugged. I knew I was making it hard for her. I felt bad, so I was making her feel bad. But she'd started it. She'd opened the box, after all.

"Schizophrenic, bipolar, manic-depressive, phobic," Bev listed. "At one time or another he's been slapped with all those labels. I think he's got a cocktail mix of antisocial conditions. All I know is when he lives away from people, he's better."

"So what—he hears voices?" I made a "crazy" face. "He sees dead people? Why didn't you just let him live in the basement like anybody else?"

"Gem—this isn't a movie. Your father has—your father had problems with things that normal—for want of a better word—people don't. When we found out I was pregnant, we both decided that it was better if he didn't live with us."

"You decided," I said.

Bev shook her hair and faced me. "Okay, if it makes you feel better, I decided."

It was Mexican standoff time. Bev was the first to crack. Her shoulders sank. She squeezed my hand.

"Chook?"

"Is that everything?" I asked.

"No that's not everything, damn it!" Bev exploded. "I want to know what's going on with you. You've been mooching around here like someone with a bullet in her backside."

"I've been outdoors," I insisted. "I've been to the creek."

"The creek doesn't count!" Bev jiggled my hand around as if she could shake my emotions free. "What about your friends? I keep expecting to come home to chaos—you three up to some intrigue . . ."

I didn't even blink. "We're having a hiatus."

Bev looked at me, despairingly. "Well, don't you want to talk about it?"

"No!" I said. "Don't you get it? I don't want to talk about anything!"

I turned my head. I didn't want Bev to see that tears were about to join our party. But maybe she guessed because she backed off then.

She said, "When you want to talk, you come find me."

# *Emergency Surgery*

Every year the television stations haul out the Christmas classics. Bev and I don't bother with *Bush Christmas*, despite the "young Nicole Kidman" factor. We will wrap presents and gasbag through Cecil B. De Mille, but when they bring on *It's a Wonderful Life*, we take the phone off the hook and watch avidly, joyously. Several hours after our "heated discussion," Bev and I were trying to act like everything was normal. We sat on the couch and nodded our heads to the opening orchestral swirl. When the front doorbell rang fifteen minutes into the film, we both groaned.

"Can we just not get that?" Whoever it was, I didn't want to see them.

But Bev hopped up from the couch. "Could be carol singers."

It was The Godmother. She spirited Bev off to the

kitchen without even saying hello. I tried to subdue the alarm bells that were ringing in my head by turning up the volume, but my mind had started wandering. I was thinking about how my life would have been different if my father had been around, but without knowing him, it was impossible to know how he might have affected me. I might have been more confident. Or I might have gone even further the other way. Hippie mum plus crazy dad didn't sound like a very promising equation.

Then I started to think about Lo—this was easier. If Lo had never transferred to our school, if the three of us hadn't glommed, who would I be now? I always thought that Lo made me bolder. So without her I would have ruled the library, while Mira and Bliss ruled the school. While I was busy erasing Lo from my personal history, Sharon must have slipped out the front door. Bev perched on the arm of the couch, reached for the remote, and switched the television off.

"Hey!" I started, but her eyes stopped me cold. "What?"

"I thought you should know that Sharon has had Mira and her parents down in her office for the better part of the week."

"Oh. Why?"

"I thought maybe you could answer that."

"Did she fail?" My voice was light. I was trying to sound concerned, and yet casual. But my pulse was already beginning to race, and I could feel my neck heating up.

"No." Bev's face was gargoylish with the lamplight behind her head. "She passed."

I forced a smile. "I'm glad. She was really worried about staying down. She studied really hard."

"Clearly. She got ninety-two for English."

"Wow!"

"Wow indeed. Sharon also told me there were disruptions during exams."

"What—the stripping thing?" I said. "That was just Mira being stupid. . . . I don't know who did the other stuff."

"Sharon thinks it was you and Lo and Mira. So is there anything you want to tell me?"

"I don't know anything!"

"Sharon's been trying to get Lo at her house. There's no answer."

That's because she's holed up in the Factory, I thought. She's probably living on trail mix and blue curaçao, researching the apocalypse, or looking for bomb recipes on the Internet.

I almost laughed. "Lo won't tell her anything."

Bev stared. My smile died on my face. "I mean, Lo doesn't know anything, either. And before you ask I don't know where she is."

"Right." Bev stood up and folded her arms. She eyeballed me for a full minute while I sank deeper and deeper into the plush cushions.

"I'm disappointed in you." She began to walk away. And suddenly I felt small and stupid. I hadn't done anything wrong, so why was I the one copping it? I wanted vindication. I didn't think it through, I just hollered at Bev's back, "Lo did it! Wrote Machiavelli round her watchband. Wrote whole essays for her. As if Mira could do it by herself."

Bev turned. "I don't believe you. Lo wouldn't do that."

"You'd believe Lo over me?"

"That's not what I meant."

I hugged my head to my knees. "You don't even know her."

There was a long silence. I was getting bad vibes and I was giving them right back. Finally my hippie mother said the one thing she vowed she'd never say: "You're grounded!"

"Where am I going to go?" I yelled. "According to you I don't even go anywhere!"

I marched out to the patio, yanking the glass door shut with all my strength. My mind had gone as black as the sky. My hands were shaking. I just wanted to punch something. And there was *Magic Man*. Judging me with his pursed lips and his monobrow. I threw a punch. I didn't expect to get anything out of it other than sore knuckles but as my fist made contact I heard a sickening rip and then looked to see *Magic Man*'s right arm dangling from a stocking. Oh God. I moved in to assess the damage. I held his wayward arm and then ever so gently pulled it toward me until it came right off. I carried the arm downstairs to my room—like a zombie with his offcuts—thinking, shit-shit-shit, I'm in for it.

**Film fact: the road to genius is paved with mistakes**

A few hours later I crept back upstairs. I checked that there was no light coming from under Bev's door, and then I went hunting for tools. I'd seen Bev make her goop up enough times—it was simple, like, just add water—but for some reason I couldn't get the consistency right. First the mix was too gluggy, then it was too runny. I dipped the end of *Magic Man*'s amputated limb into the mix and then tried twisting it back into its socket. I dipped and double-dipped, but it was no good. The thing wouldn't hold. My mother really was an artist! I sat on the ground and stared up at the monolith, my mind choppy with panic. *Magic Man* was more than a sculpture—he was a symbol! A broken *Magic Man* was like a broken heart or home or hope! I had to think laterally. I had to be resourceful.

I grabbed a wire hanger from the laundry and doubled it over to make an inner bridge between errant limb and bereft socket. Then I wound a roll of gaffer tape around the joint. Shoulder to bicep. Around and around, like forty times. Then I dipped paper scraps in the goop and started layering them over the tape to hide my bogus join. Then I stood back and took stock. So now his arm was back on, but his shoulders were uneven. I began layering the other shoulder to match the broken one. I put layer upon layer upon layer upon layer. And his shoulders were already so big to start with! By the end, I was goop-strewn and exhausted and *Magic Man* looked like a Muscle Beach hulk.

I went down to my room and unearthed the gaudiest,

most Pucci-esque, seventies-silky scarf I could find and fixed it around *Magic Man*'s neck—a cravat of sartorial splendour. As dawn rolled over the manna gums I looked at my handiwork and felt proud. I had made a good thing out of a bad thing . . . out of a good thing. I was tired.

# *Deliverance*

I woke up to the dulcet tones of my mother grunting and hollering outside my door like a farm animal in stocks.

"Gem—are you still in bed?"

"Yes."

"Well get up! You're supposed to be at work. Roger rang."

"I thought I was grounded."

"That doesn't mean you can shirk your responsibilities."

I was awake. My hair was greasy and I smelled like old sheets.

"What have you got against the door? Open up, Gem!"

"I've got no clothes on," I shouted.

"Well, hurry up and get dressed. You're not Marilyn Monroe."

Silence, but I could tell she hadn't left yet.

"Have you got someone in there?" She was using her it's-okay-we're-all-adults voice.

"No," I groaned, muttering to myself, "I wish."

"I'll wait upstairs."

While I searched for something to wear, I felt a weird rush of oxygen that culminated in the giggles. I stopped for a minute and studied myself in the mirror. Work meant Dodgy. But despite everything, I felt cool. It was like the worst stuff had happened, and now I could just get on with it. I threw on my jeans and a short-sleeved Western shirt. I crouched before the mirror, dabbed on gloss, panda-upped my eyes, and tied my hair in two bunches.

My eyes fell on the camera bag. It had been sitting by the door since Lo brought me home from the party. I peeked inside. Everything was there: camera, notebook, videotapes, and the card with Marco's phone number. "MARCO DIX—DISASTER!" I picked it up and smiled. A plan was forming. I donned dark Jackie O. sunglasses to add a touch of the untouchable to my outfit and moved out into the daylight.

*Magic Man*'s cravat was so super-shiny I was surprised the bowerbirds hadn't nicked it for a nest. There was no way Bev could have missed it. And yet she hadn't sounded that mad at me.

She was at the kitchen bench, peeking at the *I-Ching*.

I stood in front of her, hunching just a little, turning my toes together. "Does it say anything about errant daughters who don't know their own strength?" I asked her.

"Hmm." Bev had a poker face. "*Deliverance*," she read aloud. "*The superior man rescues the lonely from moral turpitude. Forgiveness is in order.*"

"It really was a mistake," I said. "And I'm so sorry about his shoulders."

"There were structural problems," Bev said matter-of-factly. Then she raised an eyebrow. "Did you know the literal translation for *papier-mâché* is chewed paper? The etymology of *mâché* is masticate. Lo told me that one."

*Great. Good on Lo.*

Bev misread my face and clucked, "Poor chook. Did you get *any* sleep last night?"

I looked at the clock. I was already an hour late. Dodgy could handle it. "Lo and Mira aren't talking to me." I spoke fast so I couldn't chicken out. "Or I'm not talking to them. At the party Dodgy and Mira dot dot dot." I gave her a leaky smile. "And Lo's been weird too. She cuts herself. *Please* don't say anything."

"Oh, Gem." Two pink spots had appeared on Bev's cheeks. "How can I *not* say anything?" She looked shocked. "What about her parents?"

"They're not even there," I admitted.

"Right." Bev closed the *I Ching*. What good was it really?

I was feeling weird, dark, spirally. "I shouldn't have said anything."

"No, you absolutely should have." She picked up her keys. "I'm taking you to work."

"I—just need to make a quick phone call." I ran to her

room and dialled Marco's number. While I was talking to him my eyes fell on the back of Bev's door. The infamous T-shirt hung there on its satin hanger. I slipped it on under my shirt, like a talisman. My inner Greer was about to be unleashed.

. . .

In the car, Bev was acting queerly calm. I didn't like it. It made me nervous.

I said, "At least you know now why I've been such a headcase."

No response.

"Mum?"

Up ahead the traffic lights were changing. Bev downshifted to second. She gave me a quick smile, then turned the volume up on the radio. "I love this song!"

Bev was croaking along to "Maggie May" when an orange VW Kombi van cut squealing in front of us. The other driver was oblivious.

"Bloody hippie!" I muttered.

I was angling for a chuckle or a twitch of my mother's lips, but Bev had pulled over to the side of the road. She was staring out the windshield. I tried to read her expression. She looked stunned, but there was something else there. "What, Mum?" I asked.

She blinked and shook the ghosts out of her head. Patted my hand. "Nothing darling, for a minute I thought . . . never mind."

I got out of the car. Outside, the landscape was eerily

still, like you'd imagine it would look after a nuclear fall-out. Bellbirds called. I almost expected to see a couple of wide-eyed wallabies watching the scene. The dust drifted back down, and I got back in the car. Bev turned the key. Betsy took a few goes to get choogling.

# Figures in a Landscape

When I entered Video Nasties, Dodgy was sitting on his stool, jiggling his feet and communing with the small screen. I unbuttoned my shirt in the doorway so that Bev's T-shirt was on full display, and then I pulled up a stool next to him. I was tough. I was a formidable woman. I wanted him to know what he was missing out on.

"Hey," I said in a neutral voice. "What's playing?"

"*Ed Wood*." Dodgy looked at me sideways. "You seen it?"

"No—I heard it's good, though."

"It's okay." Dodgy nodded. There was no dimple today, and he had a new crop of angry zits on his upper lip.

He pressed pause and explained, "Johnny Depp's just revealed his transvestite self to Sarah Jessica Parker. She's jealous because he looks better in a sweater than she does."

I permitted only the faintest trace of a smile.

We watched the movie in silence. Outside, Christmas shoppers stampeded the strip, but Video Nasties was tomb-quiet.

When it was my turn, I wandered around the shop selecting bosomy womeny period dramas: *Pride and Prejudice*, *Sense and Sensibility*, *Portrait of a Lady*, *Ethan Frome*. I bundled them up on the counter.

Dodgy groaned. "I could do without the Merchant Ivory revival."

"You want something more contemporary? More real, maybe?" This came out sharper than I'd wanted it to. And now Dodgy really looked at me. He looked in my eyes, and then he looked at my T-shirt. He smiled, but it was crooked. He looked like he'd been caught out.

I reached into my camera bag and pulled out the tape of Bliss's party. I put it in the machine and pressed play.

"For your viewing pleasure . . ."

"What is this?" Dodgy asked. And then the familiar faces flashed by.

"Oh." He was starting to go red at the neck. Good. Suffer.

"Hold on . . ." I fast-forwarded past Mira's strip and the long static stretch from when I passed out. Dodgy was jiggling his feet harder now. He'd run if I gave him half the chance.

And there it was. I pressed play. The dark gazebo suddenly spotlit. Mira and Dodgy. Fractious humping and then the shock on their faces.

I wasn't prepared for the punch of pain at seeing it again.

Even Dodgy had gone pale and quiet.

I tilted my head and tried to be an impartial observer. Dodgy and Mira were no longer people I knew. They were characters, figures in a moving landscape. So why did watching it hurt so much?

I heard Dodgy swallowing. He wasn't going anywhere.

I rewound and played the scene again. Slo-mo, this time. The sound was muffled, like white noise, so I gave it my own voiceover.

"You know, when I first met you I thought you were a dick. So patronising—all your Bergman this and Cassavetes that. And then, do you remember that day I wasn't supposed to be working, and I came in and you were watching *Malibu Bikini Shop*? You were so embarrassed, but that was when I started to like you. I stopped caring that your skin was bad and you looked like you got dressed in the dark. I thought we had a connection. Our 'moment' in the stockroom—I even thought that was something. But now I'm thinking, I could have been anyone."

I stopped the video and stood up. "You're not special enough for me," I told him. Dodgy was staring at the floor. He didn't say a word.

"Wow," I said. "That was dramatic."

A strangled sound came from deep in his throat.

"I'll need to hang on to your camera for a bit longer." I smiled at him, bright and dark at the same time. "I'm really getting my chops down."

"Sure," he squeaked.

"And I spoke to Marco about using the TAFE edit suite. He's fixed it with one of the lecturers, so you don't need to do anything."

I ejected the tape and put it in my camera bag.

"I'm going there now. Call it a long lunch." I slung the bag over my shoulder, gave him a matey arm-punch, and walked out the door, feeling better than I had since . . . well, forever.

# Party People
## Configurations

The TAFE edit suite was a windowless cell that contained computer monitors, dusty VCRs, complicated consoles, and a student lecturer-hottie named Tony.

Tony had a dirty-blond ponytail, a winky eye, and a crinkly smile. He talked me through the process of linear editing—that is, tape to tape—and then left me alone. The problem with linear is that you can't go back and stick in scenes willy-nilly—that's insert editing. This meant that I had to watch everything first and get the order solid before committing anything to tape. I had my notebook on my lap, pen poised to log the scenes and make an editing plan. I wasn't sure what I wanted. Or even what I had.

I could tell straightaway that *The F-Word* wasn't up to scratch. The script was crap, the acting sucked, my hand was too shaky, and Mira was all "look-at-me, look-at-me." It was laughable.

I put in the tape of party footage.

Mira's strip was nothing compared to the reactions around her. In fact, after a while, I realised that what was going on in the background was much more interesting than the composed scenes in our Ug film. That long static stretch after I'd passed out with the camera on my lap—that was transport! More than just plumber's crack and exposed G-strings. It was awkward hands gesturing, grasping, and falling; foreign hips bumping together, friends brushing past each other; it was fights starting and relationships ending; it was a fat kid stuffing his face with chips; a girl smoking like she knew how; and a whole comedy show of tragic dance moves. All these party people configurations. The camera saw them, even if I was dead to the world. Maybe I wasn't much of a director, but I knew gold when I saw it. The party footage was random and real. And with a little bit of work, it would become my first proper film.

. . .

I was halfway through when Tony came back in. He watched with me. I didn't mind. I felt like a professional.

"This is great," he said. "It's like social chaos."

"I didn't tell them to do any of it."

"No, but you captured it. What else have you got?"

I thought about it. "I've got lots of nature shots," I told him. Then I had an idea. I said it straight out, without worrying first that it might be stupid. "Could I do something like have the nature shots interspersed? Then it would be like animal nature and human nature all together."

Tony grinned. "We're all animals, yeah?"

I nodded, liking that he took me seriously. Liking him.

He said, "You should check out the library for—"

"Stock footage!" I spoke over him excitedly. "Bears fighting! Boxing kangaroos!"

Tony said, "Crazy party."

My eyes flicked back over to the screen. The windsock thief was dancing abstractly. Good-looking girls laughed all around him. The idea came to me wrapped up in a ribbon. I said to Tony, "That party was like distilled Darwinism. Survival of the fittest."

He looked at me. "You're not a student here, are you?"

"Not yet."

.   .   .

I stayed for five hours and came away with three dubs of a tight 45-minute film. Tony called it a "fractured narrative." I called it "lifestuff." When I thought back on my definition of an Underground film, I realised I'd matched it exactly. My film was non-mainstream. It was confrontational. There was no way a viewer could watch it without having to think. And something else: Tony suggested I come back in the New Year for some pointers on insert editing. Not so much a date as an affirmation. If ever there was an award for a day of emotional upendedness, today would have won it hands down. My Dodgy days were done with.

.   .   .

It had felt a bit weird catching the train in on my own— no Lo making up stories about the other passengers, no Mira, sitting with her legs apart, tormenting business-men and nerd boys alike. But on the train ride home I was buzzing. I had *Notes from Underground* on my lap, and I was looking at the faces of the other passengers. How was it that every single person had a world in their head—of dreams and troubles—that was different from mine?

I suddenly felt like I wanted to know everyone—ordinary people, sucker peers, even the guy in the Nickel-back T-shirt booming into his mobile phone. I'd been closing myself off from so much, and it stood to reason that if you block out the bad stuff then maybe the good stuff won't get through either. I had a villain's line in my head—*We are not so different you and I*—Marco had practically said it to me and I'd laughed at him. I wasn't laughing now. And I wasn't feeling villainous. I was feel-ing proud. For one thing, I, Gem Gordon, had sat in a small room with a strange guy for five hours, and he'd liked my stuff. And for another, I had come to the realisa-tion that art could make up for everything shitty. It sounds sucky, but it's the truth.

# A Grand Revolving Door

Christmas was in two days, and I was on the loose. Bev had lifted my grounding after I told her I hadn't yet bought her (or Sharon) a Christmas present. I tackled Sharon first. At the secondhand bookshop I found a short-story collection by a South American magical realist for the bargain price of two dollars. Then, as a sweetener, I picked up a couple of generic Third World friendship bands. If my future was in Sharon's hands, it couldn't hurt to do a spot of palm licking.

Bev was trickier. I spent a solid hour inside Inez Wisdom's Esoteric Emporium, considering her range of crystals. The amethyst headband for boosting third-eye power was too expensive, so I settled for a gift voucher for Bev to get her chakras realigned.

After that, I bought myself a salad roll and ambled along the strip with my director's eye open. The atmosphere was manic. The soothing AM "street music" (local council initiative to calm hooligan activity) didn't make a dent. Down by the river reserve the grass was cool and the breeze sultry; flies were in abundance. I charged the camera and took in my surroundings: a muumuu-clad old woman threw her sandwich crusts to the wind. She kept looking from the scraps to the sky but no ducks came. A bunch of shiny-happy people were playing hackey sack, a terrier yipped at their ankles, narrowly avoiding death by Keds. A girl not much older than me was sitting on a blanket changing her baby's nappy. Her face was blank as she went through the routine. She placed the soiled biz in her handbag and lifted the baby to the sky—their squeals of joy went back and forth.

From my position under a knotty pine, the sunshine bathed my feet. I found myself thinking, *Moments like these are the best.* Watching the world go by, wondering when to jump in, knowing I could at any time. In her hippiest moments, Bev says we are all connected. It's a Sufi thing. Like, we're all the one spirit. Ommmmm. That's cold comfort when you set store by the fact that you're different from everyone else. It's better to think that we're all different, but we're also all people and people have to live together—unless you're Marlon Brando and own your own island. Or unless you're my father.

· · ·

I scoffed my salad roll and started for the river, holding the camera at my hip, recording the rustling foliage, my boots stepping over gnarled tree roots, scattered sunlight, the foam that roamed the river's face. I was a film commando! I'd read about this technique on moviestalk.net—hipshot filming meant seeing the world at a different level—because even the most attentive director can miss things. I pointed the camera along the water's edge and listened to the bellbirds squeak their song. Just as I was thinking about how calm it was, how nice it would be to just fold in, a rock smashed the river's face, splashing water on me, and, more worryingly, on my lens. Upriver, not three feet away, Mira, Lau, Alita, Cola, J-Roam, and Marco were lumped on the bank.

I lowered the camera—had they been aiming for my head? I'd never really had enemies before. Disdain from assorted sucker peers, sure, but this? I had a vision of the future: me as the school pariah. My only social outlet: Christians and exchange students.

At least Marco was smiling at me. Marco couldn't hate anyone. He greeted me with his hand out. "Orson Welles!" he lisped. "Awesome!"

"Hi, Marco. What's up?" I looked behind him to where Mira was sitting on a stump. She was smoking a cigarette and laughing too hard at something J-Roam had said. I noticed she had a proprietary hand on his thigh. What would Lo have to say about *that*?

The transformation of Lau Warren and Alita Bean from nerdburgers to Ug whores was complete. Lau was wearing an op-art dress with Doc Martens. She had a white streak in her hair, Morticia-ish. She was smoking too—if she could have, she would have had one in each hand, I was sure. Alita Bean had gone more garden variety goth. She was wearing a wine-coloured crushed-velvet bodice with a long black skirt—her white face barely visible under her mass of dyed black hair. Seeing their pose gave me pause. I had a sudden image of a grand revolving door. Lau and Alita were going in. I was just leaving. I wondered if I'd ever be in sync.

"Yo G-," J-Roam called out. "Seen Lo? I done busted her crib but dat bitch is ghost."

I shook my head. Mira had a haughty expression on her face. Whether it was aimed at me or just because J-Roam had mentioned his ex-paramour I couldn't tell. But there was something sulky in her stance that made me smile. Mira was the kid at the milkbar who wanted *all* the lollies. My smile confused her. J-Roam started kissing her neck, and she let him, watching me all the while, with her brow bunched and her bottom lip in a twist.

"Should I give her a flyer?" I heard Lau ask.

Mira ignored her.

"I'll give her a couple."

Lau handed me some pieces of paper. I looked down at a photocopy of Andy Warhol's *Self-Portrait*—the one where his hair's all crazy—with a speech bubble that read: IT'S-A-HAPPENING NYE. DRESS TO IMPRESS. On the back was a map of the river reserve with an *X* next to the Community Centre.

"Cool, huh?" Alita enthused.

I folded the flyer. It crossed my mind that they'd co-opted *my* cool. But strangely, I didn't care. It was my turn to ask, "So what's going to happen?"

Lau looked at Alita who looked at Marco who looked at Mira who looked at J-Roam. Then they each took turns to inspect the ground, the sky, the trees, their hands, their cigarette butts. Only Marco acknowledged me with a smile in his eyes. I matched it. They had no idea. They needed Lo to look up to, and Lo wasn't there.

I said, "I guess if you get the crowds, the Happening will take care of itself."

Marco went all a'wobble. "It's a dis-*as*-ter!" he intoned.

Mira stepped forward. "It's *not* a disaster. We're still in the planning stages. One thing's for sure though, we're going to need the film." She put her hand out in a bitchy queen pose.

"What film? *The F-Word*?" I started laughing. "I don't think you want anyone to see that."

Mira threw a quick glance back at her brethren, then she grabbed my wrist and marched me several steps away from them. Once we were out of earshot she minimised her cool, her face was anxious.

"Did you tell Mincy about the cheat suit?" she asked. "Did you do it because of Dodgy?"

"I didn't tell her anything. I didn't have to."

Mira sucked her bottom lip.

"Come on, Mira—she knew! You got a ninety-two for English! You've never scored higher than sixty. Did they kick you out?"

"What do you think?"

"I think the strip probably didn't help."

Mira paused, then giggled. "It was funny, though, wasn't it?"

I didn't say anything. The first strip had been funny, but the strip at the party had been something else. I felt like there were two Miras—she was a different person when she was around Lo.

"What about Lo?" I asked. At the mention of her name, Mira reared up. She took her deputy role seriously. She said, "Lo's parents came back and put her in lockdown. She's been kicked out too. But she was going to drop out anyway, so it doesn't count. School can't teach her anything anymore."

"But is she okay?"

Mira nodded. "She's planning her escape." Her face softened and she smiled, this time it was a true smile, the flop-mouthed Mira of old. "Are you guys going to make up?"

I shook my head.

"But what about the Happening? We still need a film."

"I'll think about it," I said with a little frown. Mira looked discouraged.

I went to leave and she grabbed my hand. "Hey, are we okay?"

"Not really." I squeezed her hand hard—not to hurt her, just to show her I was serious.

"I'm sorry that all that, you know . . ."

I waited. Maybe her apology would blossom into something dignified.

"But hey!" She gave me a cutesy smile. "It was just Dodgy."

I shook my head and looked at her sadly. "You know it wasn't." And she let go of my hand and let me walk away.

# THE DIZZINESS OF
## FREEDOM

# Group Hug

On Christmas morning—*early* morning, my alarm clock winked 4:42—I bolted upright in my bed in a horror-movie panic. Something weird was afoot. I listened to the silence and shivered as the little licks of fear grew.

I got out of bed, threw on my robe, and raced up the patio stairs. I yanked the door thinking, *Please, please, please let everything be all right*. Inside, I tiptoed through the darkness to the front of the house and peered through the leadlight panel. Christmas equals weirdness. I always think about how it's supposed to be a happy time but, really, everything feels desperate, bright, and forced. People in the street have faces like grids. And the idea of a fat guy coming down your chimney is pretty creepy, when you think about it.

I heard a clanging sound. There was a light at the end of our drive. It was coming from a Kombi van. I couldn't see the colour, but I was laying bets it was orange. The curtains were drawn and there was a shadow tinkering around inside.

I rushed to Bev's room and sent her stack of night-reading scattering all over the floor. I stormed her bed and clutched at her under the covers.

"Christ!" she shrieked. "Gem, what is it?"

"There's someone outside," I whispered.

"What?"

"That van is in the driveway."

Bev struggled to a sitting position and switched her bed-side lamp on. "What van? What are you talking about?"

"The van, Mum, the Kombi! From the other day."

"What—oh." She stared at me, and then she rubbed her eyes and threw the covers aside. My mother as Woman of Action. She was pulling her tracksuit pants on. She seemed annoyed rather than frightened. Her head emerged from her poncho.

"I guess it is Christmas," she said, frowning. "Techni-cally."

I followed her out to the hall, and then out the front door, two paces behind. Bev's Ugg boots stomped through the gravel. She went right up to the van and rapped smartly on the side window.

I shrank back to the safety of shadows.

. . .

When the door of the van slid open, it sounded louder than bombs. His beard came first, then his face surrounded by a halo of grey-grizz. He drew the curtain aside and stepped out. He reached for Bev and took her hands. They stood staring into each other's eyes, and I thought about how if this were my movie, a disco soundtrack would kick in now and they would dance donuts just like John Travolta and his posh bird in *Saturday Night Fever*. As if things weren't surreal enough.

I knew who he was, of course, and I didn't feel afraid. I just felt weird. Like all of this was happening to someone else and I was watching the action from above. But maybe this is how directors are supposed to see the world, not as part of it, just taking it all in. I walked a few steps forward, into the light. Bev turned to me and said, "Gem, this is Rolf. This is your father."

He was extremely tall and skinny. He looked like if he bent too far forward or back his spine would snap. He was long of cheekbone and short of teeth, not scary but not entirely comforting either. His hair was amazing, like a fuzzy boom mike. Rolf—my father—was wearing faded denim jeans, super high-waisters, circa 1992, and a long-sleeved top. His clothes hung strangely on him, like he'd bought them from a mail-order catalogue. He came toward me with his arms akimbo, and I felt a nervous giggle on the rise. Bev walked with him. They were going for a group hug.

I let them embrace me. I felt cold, passive, sickish. Bev was cooing into my hair and Rolf was saying, "I'm psyched, I'm so psyched," and I was trapped in a pocket of air underneath their claim. I felt the telltale sweats and tremors of a spew coming on, so I ducked and escaped. I made it inside to the bathroom, just. Afterward, I rested my chin on the cold tap and studied my eyes in the vanity mirror. When I was a little mongrel pup, I used to hassle Bev about my DNA—asking her which bits I got from whom. Bev said I had her temperament and Rolf's eyes and there they were: dilated pupils, purplish shadow-bags, intimations of dread and all. But Bev had been holding back. I could see myself in Rolf's lankiness, in his awkward stance and his hesitations. I mean, really, just give me a fake beard and some bad jeans and there you have it: Rolf Gordon, circa 1989, back when one Gem Gordon wasn't even the faintest freaking glimmer.

. . .

Bev gave me a sedative. My mother actually gave me a sedative and swaddled me in sleeping bags on the couch. They stayed in the kitchen, talking low against the hum of the refrigerator. The last thing I remember hearing before I went to sleep was my father saying, "It's true, it's all true—the bright light, your life flashing past. The plane came down and I-I don't even know how they got me out."

Or maybe it was a dialogue from a movie—such things don't happen to ordinary people, do they?

**Film fact: Movies are where the real world and fantasy collide—some directors never make it back.**

# CESSNA (A Gem Gordon Concern)

**INT.: TOP-SECRET FEDERAL GOVERNMENT OFFICE—DAY**

**CHIEF SOAMES** is seated behind his handsome hardwood desk. Filing cabinets and a whiteboard with photographs and other evidence adorn the walls. We see the back of SPECIAL AGENT GEM GORDON'S head as Soames words her up on her latest case.

**CHIEF SOAMES**
Recognise this guy?

He tosses a photograph desultorily across the desk. GG picks it up. The photograph shows a hippie-ish guy standing at a podium speaking to a massive audience.

**GG**
Is the pope Catholic?

**CHIEF SOAMES**
Rolf Gordon, AKA HunterGatherer, anarchic poet,
and revolutionary.

**GG**
The man was behind the 1997 Word Riot. The
one where—

**CHIEF SOAMES**
That's right. The one where he exposed Nazi
sympathiser Herr Brughelhoffen by way of an
ingenious contemporary haiku.

**GG**
(reverent)
*The Coach and Horses Hotel*
*Hides a monster, His hands*
*stained with more than chicken parma*

**CHIEF SOAMES**
Very nice.
Now—what do you make of this?

Soames tosses over another photograph—this
time a black-and-white of a severed ear.

**CHIEF SOAMES**
Our "genius" has been kidnapped. We have the coordinates. I want YOU to bring him home.

**GG**
(*A cool smile*)
It will be my pleasure. See you Tuesday, Chief.

Even Chief Soames—a happily married and well-respected federal agent—cannot resist staring at GG's derriere as she strides efficiently out of his office.

**EXT.: SKIES OVER TASMANIA—NIGHT**
An unmarked Cessna airplane storms across Tasmanian skies.

**INT.: CESSNA—NIGHT**
GG is at the wheel. In the seat behind her is Rolf Gordon with a bandage around his left ear. He looks panic-stricken over his shoulder every few seconds.

**GG**
Relax, Mr. Gordon. We've lost them.

GG flies on, smiling as she speaks.

**GG**
I have to say, I have admired you for a long
time, Mr. Gordon. I studied your work in high
school.
(her face goes misty as she quotes him)
*"Swiftly so, falling ever*
*The lark of lost lovers*
*Crepe-wing and crystal talon"*

**ROLF GORDON**
I'm impressed. I didn't know they had my
texts at Superhero High.

**GG**
I'm no superhero, Mr. Gordon. I'm just a girl
who believes in justice.

Rolf Gordon looks significantly at his saviour. His face changes as recognition hits.

**ROLF GORDON**
This will sound strange . . .

**GG**
Go on . . . I'm all ears . . .
(*she glances at his bandaged head*)
Sorry.

**ROLF GORDON**
I, too, have been wanting to meet YOU for a
long time.

GG looks confused. Rolf Gordon tries to explain.

**ROLF GORDON**
If only the circumstances were different . . .
I ah, I, well, come on man, out with it. GG,
I'm your—

Suddenly there is a commotion as the Cessna
hits an air pocket. Rolf cries out in fear,
but with GG behind the wheel, he needn't be
afraid.

**GG**
(above the mad whir of the engine)
Sorry Rolf, we're going to have to make a
crash landing. Put your head between your
knees and breathe deeply, BREATHE DEEPLY!

There is a loud squeal as GG brings the plane
down. Cabin flotsam flies above their heads.
She manages to land in an open field to an audience of blasé sheep.

**GG**

Now—what was it you were going to tell me?

Rolf Gordon weeps with relief. GG is magnificent. Her hair only slightly rumpled in the fray. Rolf Gordon whispers in her ear. She looks stunned.

**GG**

You're my wha-?

She flings her arms around his neck, rejoicing.

**GG**

Oh, Daddy!

THE END

# Christmas Presence

In the morning, at a more civilised hour, I hid my face under my blanket and watched Rolf at play. He was resting on the couch with a cup of hot water (who drinks hot water?), and he was staring at the television, fascinated. This would have been fine if it had actually been switched on.

"You can watch it," I heard Bev say. "It'll just be cartoons, though."

"I don't want to wake Gem." His voice was low and gravelly.

"When was the last time you watched TV?" Bev asked. And her voice had a bit of a kick in it, like she was nervous. I inched a little farther under my blanket and breathed softly.

Rolf said, "I think I can remember the Gulf War."

"Oh," Bev joked, "everyone knows that was just a movie."

Rolf didn't laugh. He looked sad. The silence between them was so excruciating that I had to step in.

"Merry Christmas." I waved my hand and said a straight-faced, "Whoo-hoo." And Rolf turned toward me with a look so keen I wanted to pull the cover straight back over my head and keep it there forever.

.   .   .

I read somewhere that all the different details and memories of your life are stored in random locations in your brain. So a big whack in the right spot can make a puritan go potty mouth or give a staunch vegetarian a jonesing for jerky. Was it brain damage or brain repair, I wondered, that could make a man suddenly focus on the fact that he had a teenage daughter?

Rolf Gordon made it sound simple. He'd had a near-death experience and he had seen the light. He'd been working as a ranger at Cradle Mountain since the early nineties—uneventful thus far—then, a month ago, a botanist from Leeds hired him to fly him to the South-West wilderness. An engine malfunction sent their Cessna nosediving to certain doom. Only somehow they both survived. See what I mean? Simple.

It sounded unbelievable, but then again, his very presence was unbelievable. For all the teasing postcards I never thought he'd actually appear. In the past, and only occasionally, I had allowed myself to magick him up, like in a movie. Sometimes he'd rock up in a limo with a backstage pass and a champagne cocktail, or he'd kidnap me after school, sweep me up in a hot-air balloon, spread his arms, and say, "This, all this is yours!" Sometimes my fantasies were more low rent: I'd bump into him in the city, he'd take me to his minimalist apartment and tell me his troubles.

My imagined father was always *above* society. Just like I thought I was above my sucker peers. I'd joked about inheriting his antisocial edge. Except—I was only just realising this—I wasn't all that antisocial. I suspected I was, as Bev liked to say, merely *impressionable*.

More than anything, I did not want my father to make an impression on me. I had come so far without him.

. . .

Now he leaned toward me, with his eyes spooky-wide.

"When the plane came down I saw you, Gem, with your mother. You were welcoming me. I have to be careful here. I don't want to sound trite but it was like a wake-up call. I just knew I had to see you."

My life as a soap . . . any minute now Ridge and Stephanie would be making an appearance to lend more gravitas to his story. I think I was supposed to say something, but I was wincing on the inside. Outwardly I nodded, then edged back a little.

If this were a normal Christmas, Bev would be wreaking havoc in the kitchen and singing Christmas carols off-key. She was in the kitchen, but she was moving like a Ninja. I lay back on the couch and rolled my head to the side like a convalescent. And then I thought of something.

"How did you know what I looked like?"

Rolf was rolling a cigarette with long, spidery fingers. He looked up, confused. "What do you mean?"

"I mean, in your vision. You've never seen me before so how did you know what I looked like?"

Rolf finished rolling his cigarette. He paused and then smiled at me. "I just knew."

"You can't smoke in here," I told him.

He looked at me in surprise. Then he sucked the roll-up to seal it and walked out to the patio. His pants were so high! His bum looked flat and squarish, like a half-filled hot water bottle. Like mine.

. . .

Bev brought over a plate of mince pies. She watched Rolf through the window—he was leaning on the patio rail, sending little smoke signals into the sky. Bev turned to me with a hopeful smile.

"So what do you think of your old man?"

"Do you really want to get into that now?"

Bev flinched and sighed. "Probably not." Then she bit into a mince pie. "I'm delaying gratification," she surmised, trying to make a joke. I gave her an annoyed glance. The only thing she was delaying was a fight. Bev looked at me worriedly. She knew. "You say a lot with a look," she told me.

We both observed Rolf smoking and touching up *Magic Man*. He seemed pretty comfortable for a complete stranger.

"So is he going to stay?" Now my voice had a crack in it. "Where's he going to sleep? Do we even want him here?"

Bev started to say something, then stopped. "I'm guessing he'll sleep in the van." She sighed. "Honey, I can't answer for you. You're your own person. But I'm not kicking him out on Christmas Day. We'll talk about it tomorrow."

"If you say so, Scarlett O'Hara."

Bev scraped back her fringe and gave me a hard look that meant, *No bullshit.* "Do you want to open your presents now or after lunch?"

"Whatever," I said. "I guess I'll get dressed."

Why wasn't there an easier way to my room? I pushed the blanket aside and marched out the front door and around the other side of the house. He would have heard me going into my room. I knew it made me look churlish. But I didn't want to pass him. I didn't want him saying any more weird shit to me. How long did it take to suck a rollie back, anyway?

# The Fugitive

At noon I heard a loud exhalation outside my door. I went out to investigate. It was The Godmother. She'd come around the side and was now contemplating the patio steps. She was wearing an African dashiki thing with gigantor purple flowers on it and carrying a cane basket full of gifts and cleanskin wines.

"It's not very Christmassy keeping the front door locked," she huffed. "Whose is the van? Have you had some kind of emergency? Don't tell me the plumbing's gone."

"Did you get that dress off Mama Cass?" I asked her.

She looked down at her dress, then up at me. "How are you anyway?"

I shrugged. "I'm okay. I'm mateless."

"Mates like those two you can do without." Sharon gave me a sympathetic smile. I didn't feel like I deserved it after listening to Lo and Mira call her Mincy all year. She wasn't so bad.

I made a gesture toward the stairs. Sharon may have wanted a private talk, but I was hungry. I let her go first. She kept talking as she climbed, wheezing intermittently.

"You did the right thing. Mira will be fine. But why didn't you tell us Lo's situation?"

I was startled—did Sharon know about her cutting?

"What do you mean?"

"Her parents were in Noojee. 'Working through their divorce,' according to Mr. Hunter."

"But Lo said they were at a conference."

"Well, you should have told me she was on her own. You should have told someone."

"What about the woman from the parish who was minding her?" I said, remembering when I called up and the timid woman answered. Could Lo have been faking it?

Sharon looked at me blankly. "There was no minder. The only reason I was able to get in touch with her parents was through the parish, and they told me that Lo's been on her own since October."

"Lo can look after herself." But even as I said it I knew it wasn't true. The look Sharon gave me said she felt the same.

"You girls are just that—girls."

Sharon rested her basket at her feet, barring me from going any further. She had on her Look of Grave Concern and was sucking the insides of her cheeks like a puffer fish.

"This is your time, Gem. You should be surrounding yourself with good folk. Smart, adventurous, bright sparks like yourself. They exist! I get that Lo might be exciting to you, but she has problems."

That wasn't exactly fair. For a long time Lo was more than exciting. She was my friend. She plucked me from obscurity and told me to embrace my weird self when everybody else was telling me to pretend it didn't exist. *Show me the bright sparks*, I wanted to say. Lo was a bright spark, the brightest.

"You're the school counsellor," I said. "Isn't that where you're supposed to come in?"

"Maybe once I could have. She's out of my hands now."

I bent down to pick up her basket. But she wasn't finished with me.

"By the way, you don't know anything about a plasma screen going missing from Bliss Dartford's house, do you?"

I shook my head no, but I had a pretty good idea who did.

Then Sharon gasped. "What happened to him?" She'd just noticed *Magic Man*. She completed a lap around him, marvelling, "He's a freak!"

"I broke his arm," I admitted.

"I don't know," she said finally. "You could have left it off. Then he would have been like the one-armed man in *The Fugitive*." She shook her head. "What do I know? Your mother's the artist."

Just over the threshold I let it slip.

"Speaking of fugitives," I said, "Rolf's here."

Sharon stopped in her tracks and stared around the room. She gave me a look so charged with surprise that I found myself thinking of silent movies, how the actor's facial expressions had to be explicit because they were the "words" that told the story. If this were my silent movie, the next scene would show Sharon hitting herself on the forehead, and a title would come up that read: "Of course! Tasmanian license plates!"

# Only the Good Things

In the kitchen, there was evidence of Bev everywhere—from the batch of mutant gingerbread men cooling on the stovetop to the suds in the sink—but the maker of the mess was nowhere to be seen. Sharon, at a loss as to what to do, had put the kettle on and was now patting her hair obsessively. I separated a Siamese gingerbread man from his twin, scoffed his head first, then began working my way down to his bulging clubfoot.

My father loped inside from the bathroom. He'd shaved his beard off and tied his frizz back into a topknot. This made him look younger and friendlier, more human. Despite the tan line on his face.

"Hello, stranger!" He held his arms out, and Sharon fell in. She was pummelling his shoulders—not angrily, but she did seem keyed up. Rolf smiled at me over her shoulder. I raised my eyebrows and kept eating. The gingerbread tasted sweet and crumbly soft. It smelled like my childhood. Bev used to pack these culinary freaks in my playlunch. She was so free form, couldn't bear the idea of cookie cutters. She could barely follow a recipe.

Sharon was doing her Inadvertent John Wayne Impersonation, asking Rolf, "What say, Pilgrim? Where have you been hiding?"

But Rolf had bigger ideas than explaining himself.

"I'll be back." He extricated himself and jogged out the front door.

Sharon breathed out, "Oh, my."

"Huh." I snorted. "That's what Bev said."

Then Bev broke up the party. She was wearing a cotton halter dress. And she was wearing lipstick. And so much rouge she looked sunburned. The only thing marring her makeover was the Santa earrings that bobbled near her jaw.

"Look at you!" Sharon cooed. "She's still got it!" She nudged my mother like a gossipy girl. "When did he turn up?"

"Last night," I cut in.

"What's he doing here?"

Bev displayed her palms. She opened her mouth to speak and then covered it with her hand. That wasn't rouge—it was emotion!

My mother was sobbing. I made a step away from the gingerbread men and toward Bev. I thought she was happy to have my father here, but obviously I'd missed something. I rubbed my hand on her back and tried to think of what to say. I couldn't bring up the change again. Bev was sniffing, she muttered something about Mercury being retrograde. I stopped myself from murmuring "*convenient*," and continued sanding her shoulders. Sharon was taking over. Sharon had bigger hands. There was more of her. Which meant she had more to give. She shepherded Mum back to her bedroom. I went to follow, Sharon gave me a look.

"Put the kettle on, love."

"It just boiled!"

"Gem—"

"Okay, okay," I muttered.

Rolf returned carrying a haversack, and I witnessed the face slide—big smile to straight line—when he realised I was the only one there.

"Where'd they go?"

I jerked my head toward the bedroom. "Bev got something in her eye."

·  ·  ·

We were marooned in the kitchen. Our centre had deserted us. I pushed the plate of gingerbread toward him, and we silently munched.

After a bit, my father nodded to his haversack. "Know what that is?" He was trying to be playful.

"A bag?"

"Well, a haversack. I call it my happy-sack. Want to know why?"

I rolled my eyes and acted like it pained me to speak. "Why?"

"Because it contains only the good things." He grinned and became the man in the stolen strip of photos, so many moons ago. I had an inkling then of "Oh, my" myself because there was everything to like in that smile. But I didn't want to like him!

"God!" I said, exasperated. "How old do you think I am?"

My father looked at me, stunned. "I was only—" but I wouldn't let him finish. I stormed off outside, down the stairs to my room. I dug around under my bed until I found my emergency cigarettes. Then I lit one up and took furious little puffs until my head hurt and I had to lie down.

# The Big Kiss-off

I drank red wine all through Christmas lunch. The elders
hardly noticed me. They had a history and they were in-
tent on revisiting it.

Bev was all charged up. Or tipsy, it was hard to tell.
Either way, she had sorted out her stumble-tongue, and
now she couldn't shut up. She was telling Rolf about her
teaching and about *Magic Man* and the Red Roof Artists
Show. She talked about the Community Centre's fifteen-
year anniversary. The memory wall was almost complete. New Year's Eve would host the big reveal. Sharon
was similarly afflicted. She focused more on global issues: fake terrorists, unfair trade, bombs, blight, bird
flu—stuff my father would have known about if he had
any connection to the now. The elders weren't ignoring
me. They just couldn't see me. All they could see was
Rolf. They reminded me of speed chess competitors. Bev

would lay down an anecdote, pause for breath, and then—
*ding*—Sharon would swoop in with her side of the story.
Once or twice Rolf tried to get me involved. What did I
like? What did I want to be? I answered him in grunts and
monosyllables.

I couldn't eat the nut roast. My stomach was a sac of
bile bobbing in a sea of beaujolais. Bev was almost fawn-
ing, and I found her behaviour confusing. Where had her
feminist ideals gone? I stared at her until she looked up.
And it seemed to me her smile was guilt-edged.

Now Rolf had his elbows on the table; he was resting
his head in his palm as he described his "rustic" shack.
"There's nothing in it but tinned food and paperbacks,"
he said. "Oh, but sometimes people give me things."

Sharon leaned in, fascinated. "What people?"

"Hikers, tourists, wanderers . . ."

"What things?"

"Socks, energy bars . . . sealing wax," Rolf joked. With
his free hand he was feeling the bobble-knit texture of the
tablecloth. I watched Bev staring rapturously at his fingers as they scratched over the fabric and then it struck
me—she was still in love with him!

What was this mysterious hold my father had on her?
He looked intense but not crazy—at least not TV-movie
crazy. He was a careful speaker, but you couldn't call him
uptight. When he smiled his face would lift and lighten—
in fact, whatever expression he wore, his eyes were always tied to it. I believed him to be honest. And it was
getting harder to find reasons not to like him.

Post-dessert, my father delved into his "happy-sack" and brought out a big, battered photo album.

"Is that what I think it is?" Bev grinned.

"Oh, please." Sharon was nearly choking. "Let the food settle first!"

I endured laughter, squeals, and sighs before excusing myself.

"No wait, Gem," Rolf said. "I want you to see these too."

"I have a headache."

Bev suddenly remembered her mum-ness. "Do you want an aspirin?"

"No." I got up from the table. I was one surly girly. Bev had a glass of wine to her lips. She nodded to me above the rim, a look that I translated as, "We'll talk later." I hoped she could see that I was feeling all sorts of weird, jealous, hostile un-Christmassy feelings. But then Sharon said something, and they all cracked up. From the next room they sounded like a laughing club. It felt horrible to be on the outside of that. I didn't qualify for membership.

. . .

I unplugged the TV and carried it down to my bedroom. While Bob Dylan wittered on upstairs about his 115th dream, I put my film in the camera and connected the leads. I had my own history, and it had nothing to do with any of them. I watched me and Lo and Mira. Who was holding the camera? Marco? Dodgy? Anyway, we three were tripping, laughing. We were connected. If only for a split second before it all went to shit. Without thinking, I picked up the phone and dialled Lo's number.

Her father answered, "Hunter house."

"Can I speak to Lo, please," I asked.

"Who is this?"

"It's Gem Gordon."

"Wait just a minute." There was shuffling and muttering and at least two minutes of dead air. My heart skipped and my hand seized. But I couldn't hang up.

"Hello?"

"Lo?" I squeaked.

There was a pause, then a drawn out, "Ye-ah?"

"It's me. Gem."

"I know. What do you want?"

"I don't know. I just rang to say Merry Christmas."

She didn't say anything.

I took a deep breath. "And I wanted to know . . . how are you?"

"I'm dandy." I heard her light up and puff into the phone. "Mincy wants to put me into some pissy self-love programme. My parents think I'm the Anti-Christ. How are you?"

"I'm having a blue Christmas," I confessed.

Lo's voice was terse. "Yeah, well, you get what you pay for." When I didn't respond she said, "And if you don't know what that means you should ask your mother."

"I get it," I said. "It's a Sufi thing." Gone were the days of Lo telling me what was what. Her snotty tone prompted me to bring up something that sounded like the big kiss-off.

"Could I get my brown dress back off you?"

Lo snorted. "Have we come to that?"

"I wanted to see you and Mira. I've got the film for the Happening."

"Awesome." Lo tapped the phone. Then she said, "My parents are on suicide watch. And Mira's trying to get the Happening happening. There's a lot to do."

"I know. But, well, couldn't you find a window?"

Lo was quiet for ages. I could practically hear her brain ticking. Finally she said, "I guess we could meet the day before."

"What time?" I asked.

"Two o'clock?"

"Okay. Cool. Can you tell Mira?"

"Yeah. Where do you want to meet?"

"HQ," I said.

"Whatever."

We both hung up. My heart was pounding out a techno beat. I had to light another cigarette just to calm it down.

# Fractured Narrative

There was a knock on my door. I opened it to find Rolf standing there with a bowl of Christmas pudding in his hand. "Can I come in?"

I stepped aside. He had to stoop under the low pine ceiling. He looked around my room, at all the paraphernalia and pieces of me.

"Wow," he said. "Wow. You've got a whole little den down here."

He sat on my bed and handed me the bowl. I put a spoonful of pudding in my mouth. "Mmm," I grunted. "Good."

"Bev said you're a big movie buff." He looked at the video camera. "You make movies?"

I nodded. I felt a bit better.

"I used to take photos. Black-and-whites." He held his hands up in a pretentious artist's pose and uttered, "Light and shade." His hands came down. "I haven't done it for a long time now."

"Why'd you stop?"

"I don't know. Actually, that's not true. I'll tell you why. In the beginning I just had one camera, but then I started accumulating: flash, light meter, tripod, lenses. I started to feel like I was carrying all this burden of . . . stuff . . . and, you know, it's okay if you have your own dark room, but I didn't want Joe Blow down at the chemist developing my vision. So one day I set up for a self-timer shot and walked back to where $X$ marked the spot, and I just kept walking."

I put my bowl down. "You don't seem that crazy," I said. "Just an observation."

His laugh was abrupt. "Who said I was crazy?"

I rolled my eyes up to the ceiling, meaning Bev. Rolf said fondly, "Ahh, she's the crazy one. One day I'll tell you the story of how we met."

He shifted on the bed next to me and focused on the screen. My film was playing from the start. Mira and Lo in cahoots. The party in progress.

"Did you do this?" Rolf asked.

I nodded and reached down to press the pause button.

"It's a fractured narrative," I told him, but it didn't feel right to use Tony's words, so I felt around for my own. "It's a sort of documentary about the poses people put on. Everyone's always trying to be so cool, but they can't maintain it. And that's when you see all this other stuff. That's when the truth comes out."

"Uh-huh." He looked at me, sort of searching my face.

"What?" I felt myself getting embarrassed.

"That scar you've got—" he pointed to the scar next to my right eyebrow. "That's from chicken-pox. When you were four, right?"

I stared at him. "Um, yeah." It felt too early in our relationship to be body mapping, but when he grabbed my two hands I let him.

"Line your fingers up," he said. I put my index fingers together.

"The one on the left is bent. That's from netball. When you were nine. You played centre and the goal attack from Narrong Primary jammed the ball up against your finger. You had to wear a splint for a month."

"How did you know that?" I asked. *This* was crazy— my father, touching my hands, telling me my memories. And what was even crazier than that was I didn't mind. I wanted to hear more.

Rolf rolled a cigarette, and then he rolled another. He passed one to me. I took it and lit it and listened.

"When you were twelve, Bev took you to Kilcunda and you nearly drowned trying to bodysurf. You told Bev that you saw God and he had a mullet and footy shorts, but that was just the surfer dude that saved you.

"When you were fourteen, you got your period and you didn't tell your mother for six months—"

"Stop!" I said, holding my hand up.

"Because you knew she'd want to document it in some way, take your picture, paint your portrait.

Because that's what she does. That's what she always did."

My jaw was on the floor. "How do you . . . ?"

My father opened the drawstring to his happy-sack and withdrew a fat stack of letters, all addressed to him in Bev's handwriting. Then he drew out another stack, and another. There were photos there too. Seventeen years' worth. Rolf had a portable version of Bev's memory wall right there in his bag.

"I know I wasn't there for any of it, but I felt like I was." He paused, then added, "For what it's worth."

"I don't understand," I said, after I'd got my breath back. "Bev never told me that she wrote to you." My mind was starting to blare. "If you wanted to know about me, why didn't you just phone us up? Or come and visit? Was it Bev?" My voice was going up, up, up. "Did she say you couldn't see me?" I felt like I'd sucked back a cone of dry ice. It filled my lungs and made my head hurt. My shoulders started to tremble and suddenly I was crying. "I don't understand."

"Your mother told you I was crazy." He rubbed his jaw and stared at me. "I have these *issues*, that's true— put me in a room with more than ten people and I start to get the shakes. I used to be a lot worse. *A lot.*" Rolf's eyes were fixed on mine. The skin around them was like rough terrain. He held my hand and said in a clear voice. "I had a drug habit, Gem. It wasn't nice and it wasn't romantic and it wasn't anything you needed in your life."

In the long silence that followed, I saw a montage of

movie images of junkies: screeching and nodding and thieving and bleeding, most of them looked like hell, but some of them—some of them were charming.

"What about now?"

"Now I'm clean, but it took . . . a long time."

"Seventeen years?"

Rolf hung his head. "I know." He sounded ashamed. "There's nothing I can say. I went away. I kept thinking I'd come and see you. But then I'd hear from Bev that you were doing so great, and I didn't want to mess that up. I'm sorry, Gem. I wish things had been different." His rollie had gone out. He stared at it for ages. I didn't say anything. I couldn't. Then he turned to me and said, "That's the facts of our existence."

I nodded, numb, and then I wiped my eyes. "I just thought you didn't want to know me."

He shook his head slowly and gave me that smile that sent Bev and Sharon hosepiping. He said, "You and me have got work to do, kiddo."

. . .

As if on cue, the pause exhausted itself and my film unfurled: on with the strip, the surreal asides from strangers, secrets caught on camera. And because I didn't know what to say to Rolf, because he'd startled me so and I didn't want to cry again but I felt like maybe I was about to, I let the film play on. We watched it together, my father and I, smoking in silence.

# *Crackers*

Later, later.

Sharon and Rolf were having a powwow in his van. Bev was having a bath. I sat on the kitchen stool and delved into my father's photo album. It was ancient, the kind with the self-adhesive paper inside that turns your memories into lifers. It had a yellowed index with numbered spaces for commentary, but only a hippie-dippy aphorism was inked in: *When I think of all that is possible, I get dizzy with freedom.*

The first few pages contained black-and-white nature shots: a dark fern gully, a massive mountain ash, a pristine beach. Impressive. Then for a few pages there were photos of faces I didn't recognize. Beardos in black jeans and patterned vests; total femmos with feather cuts, sans makeup, breasts wayward under tight T-shirts; people at kitchen tables with big wooden salad bowls and Chianti bottles; hairy seventies uni-types at demonstrations wielding BAN URANIUM signs.

My eyes widened on various photos of two couples. The pictures had been taken on the same day in a riveresque backdrop that looked like home. I recognised Bev immediately. She was resplendent in a Hawaiian-print sundress. Sitting next to her was my father. How handsome he was before he stopped eating processed food! He wore jeans and a necklace made out of twigs. They looked in love, all happy smiles and hands-on. I got a weird feeling in my stomach looking at them—a sort of suspense.

I dragged a nail along the edge of the photographs.

Who were the other two? I felt like I'd dreamed these scenes before. A cool guy in baggy combat trousers and dark shades sat next to a beautiful sun-kissed girl in a bikini top and cutoffs. I tried to see if there was anything written on the back of the photograph, but it was fixed too tight. I let the plastic fall back and smoothed out the air bubbles before turning to the last page. The beautiful girl stared up at me. Her hair was long and strawberry blonde; her skin was peachy; her teal-blue eyes were wide; and her lips were parted as if she was just about to respond to something remarkable.

Bev sidled up in a cloud of ylang-ylang. "She was a looker all right."

"Who is she?"

"Can't you tell?"

I shook my head.

"Really?" She gave me her Wise Old Woman Look.

"I honestly have no idea."

"It's Sharon," Bev said. "She's about your age there."

"You're kidding—Sharon?"

"Uh-huh." Bev broke off some gingerbread and tried to act idle.

"But she's beautiful!" I burst out.

"Uh-huh." Bev smiled maddeningly. "She's still beautiful."

"Oh, come on, I mean she's *beautiful*. What happened?"

Bev wiped her hands on her pyjama pants. She looked at the clock. "Oops. It's not Christmas anymore."

"Mu-um," I whined. I turned back a few pages. "Who's Mr. Cool? Was he her boyfriend?"

Bev stopped wiping her hands. She studied the photo, and her merry look folded into sadness. "Yes. His name was Art Pepito. He was your Dad's best friend too. Now he was crackers." She put the plug in the sink, turned the taps on, added dishwashing liquid, and looked around for dirty dishes.

"You already did the dishes, Bev," I reminded her.

"Did I? Oh, dear, I must be getting Alzheimer's." She picked up a tea towel and started drying the cutlery with her back to me. She never dried the cutlery!

"So what happened to him?" I asked.

"Well. He died."

"How did he die?" I pressed.

"He OD'ed," Bev said. "Sharon never got over it. None of us did."

I ran my nail under the photo album's ring binding. Up and down, down and up. Up and down, down and up . . .

"Rolf told me why he stayed away," I said.

"I know."

I had to ask. "Are you still in love with him?"

Bev twisted the tea towel into what could have been a noose. "I'll always be in love with him. But that doesn't change anything. It's funny. When you get to be as old as we are, sometimes you think you used to be someone else . . ." Her voice drifted off. She looked at me, and it was as if we made a silent promise to each other: we'd talk about it. We'd talk about it all. When we were both feeling strong.

Bev was hanging on to that tea towel for dear life. I grabbed one end of it and gave it a playful tug.

"Inez Wisdom says a person changes radically every seven years," I told her. "I can feel myself changing at the moment. It's like the wheel's turning round—*click, click, click*. By the time I'm twenty-one, who knows where I'll be?" I blathered on. "I mean there's no way I am the same person I was at fourteen, right?"

"You were a delight at fourteen. You were industrious and committed and very sweet."

"I was a dork," I insisted.

Bev's eyes floated upward. "Come on, tiger. Help me make the coffee."

# Hippie Moment

In the Boxing Day dawn, Bev took a moment to consult the *I-Ching* with me. I closed my eyes and silently asked the oracle how to deal with my prodigal father. But the answer seemed to have more to do with my friends than my family. It was the hexagram *Sui—Following.*

I read aloud: *"What you seek becomes you through following."*

*"Que?"*

"Well," Bev probed, "what do you seek?"

"Um . . . I just want things to get easier," I said. "You know how in silent films you have to get by with what you're looking at?"

"I'm not sure I follow."

"Sorry, I was thinking filmic-ly." I stopped and started again. "I want life to be clear. And I want to make a truly great film. And I want someone cool to hang out with."

"It says here you have to *step higher than the shallow and inferior*," Bev noted.

"Oh, that's already happened."

I read on. "*The distinguished man must journey again. This is natural and right. . . .* Do you think you could call Rolf distinguished?"

Bev took my hand in hers. "Gem—I want to ask you something. It's important to me. About your father. Do you think it's enough that he's here now, or do you feel like you've been cheated of something?"

I thought about it. I didn't miss the ghost. "I don't think so," I said. "He's better than the idea I had of him. Do you feel cheated?"

Bev shook her head and smiled. "I think you and I have had a whale of a time. You were my little bean, and you've grown up great and smart and beautiful. I wouldn't have done it any differently. Or well, a couple of things . . ."

I thought about that for ten long seconds before deciding, "Me too."

We had a big ol' hippie hug and a spot of tearing up. When Bev released me I said, "I should have asked more questions."

"Oh, honey!" Bev's face was a marriage of the crestfallen and the comic. "If you don't ask the questions, you'll never get the answers."

# Gem Gordon's Top Five

**Film fact: Movies let us know that we are not alone.**

Over the next few days I spent quality time with Rolf Gordon.

I took him along the strip first. Video Nasties was closed for Christmas break, but I smuggled him in with my key and showed him my top five. This was the personal film history that I never got to share with Dodgy, but Rolf was a wonderful audience. I led him through the eras.

*How to Marry a Millionaire*—A three-girls film where they all live happily ever after. Marilyn Monroe, Lauren Bacall, and Betty Grable are models sharing a New York penthouse in order to snag a silver fox. It's kind of immoral but lots of fun and not that far away from femmo thinking.

*Chinatown*—This film made me understand what all the fuss about Jack Nicholson was about—emphasis on *was*. *Chinatown's* storyline is long and winding and every time I watch it I forget what's coming. But when it gets there, it's always worth it.

*Gas Food Lodging*—The adventures of a teenage girl who lives with her single mum in a trailer in the desert. She loves a long-forgotten Mexican movie star and can't relate to her peers. In other words (Inez Wisdom's) she is my "spiritual twin."

*Vertigo*—"This film has the longest screen kiss in the history of movies," I told Rolf. "That was a while back—someone's probably beaten the record by now." I pictured Dodgy and felt a small twinge for the death of romance.

*Withnail and I*—Two unemployed actors, Withnail (Richard E. Grant), a paranoid, self-absorbed alcoholic maniac, and "I" (Paul McGann), our somewhat timid narrator, swindle their way into a country home and barely make it out alive. Millions of people loved this movie, but it still seemed custom made for outsiders—and perfect for me and my father.

I held up the cover. "This is the one we're going to watch." Rolf cooked his hands. "I'm ready," and we took our seats behind the counter. I loved watching Rolf watching *Withnail and I*. He laughed his head off right up until the end—and then we both cried when Withnail gave his devastating soliloquy in the rain at Regent's Park.

Afterward we discussed how "I" didn't have an inch of Withnail's talent, but Withnail's personality was so impossible and self-destructive that it eclipsed all hope.

"How come the mediocre always seem to get the rewards?"

I could ask this stuff of my father. I was starting to learn he was great at abstracts.

"It doesn't always go that way. And rewards aren't really the point, are they?"

"They *feel* like the point," I said.

"I used to worry that I'd never amount to anything," Rolf confessed. "I sometimes think that's the real reason I stopped taking pictures."

"But you wrote haikus."

"Word pictures," he conceded, screwing his face up. "Not quite the same thing. Which reminds me . . ."

He reached into his happy-sack and pulled out a copy of his book of haikus—*Hunter-Gatherer*.

"There's only fifty of these in existence," he said. "It's not rare. Just self-published." I turned it over. The cover was worn rice-paper thin. It showed a pen-and-ink sketch of Rolf's profile, signed by Art Pepito, Sharon's long-dead lover. The book felt like treasure.

"You're in it," Rolf told me.

"I'm in it?"

"Beneath carefully constructed layers of metaphor."

"Right." I put the book in my back pocket. For the rest of the day I could feel it there, radiating.

We walked along the river. I filmed Rolf as he spotted native birds and flowers and told me their secrets. Our art versus life discussion continued.

"It's funny," Rolf said. "All these fleeting images, every one of them is a moment that leads on to another moment. Everything you see affects you. And everything that affects you, affects the people you affect."

"It sounds like a riddle."

"I guess it is."

. . .

We were scoffing red licorice strips at the river reserve when a freak shower forced us into the council information shelter. I read the graffiti while Rolf perused the community notices.

"What about this—TAFE film night—talks, screenings—it's tonight!"

"I don't know," I wavered. It was the talk Dodgy was giving. "I thought you wanted to watch that documentary on SBS. And anyway, don't crowds make you sweaty?"

"We can tape the documentary, and I can take a towel. I want to do something with my daughter." He ripped the notice down and gave me a quizzical look. "Why the *umming* and *ahhing?* This looks right up your alley."

"I don't know—I just . . . I was invited to it already," I admitted.

"Terrific!"

"But I don't like the guy who invited me."

Now he looked at me, his brow creased a thousand times over in sympathy. "Ex-boyfriend?"

"Hardly."

"So, stuff him! We'll all go. As a family. It will be *an event*."

"But you don't understand, he's giving a talk."

"All the better! Be a vocal participant:"—he cupped his hand and droned through it—"Boring! Cliché! Bull-shit!"

I had to laugh.

If this was just a kernel of my father's personality, it was the best bit. This was my *It's a Wonderful Life* moment. Maybe with Rolf in my life there wouldn't have been any of this soft-cheese psyche shit. Maybe the Bliss Dartfords of the world would never have made a dent. Maybe the top of the triangle would have always been pressing into my palm.

"Okay," I said. "But you've got to do something about your jeans."

"These? What's wrong with them?"

"Hello? How high the waist?"

My father looked down at his high-waisters and then up at me. "You teenagers worry about the weirdest shit."

There was something else on the notice board. A row of stickers. Andy Warhol's fright wig. "IT'S A HAPPEN-ING! DRESS TO IMPRESS" I'd almost forgotten about it, but now I smiled. My mind was beginning to turn. Mira had risen to the challenge. She was putting the word out. Would the Happening turn into an un-Happening? Whatever *did* happen, I wanted to be there to document it. I was thinking filmic-ly and I was predicting gold!

# Look to the Father

"In his films, Nicholas Ray gave us outsiders and rebels. *They Live by Night*, they live in the margins. They see a brighter world, but they cannot access it . . ."

Thus said Roger "Dodgy" Brick, film student and video store lackey, at the close of his address. I had to admit, I was impressed. I'd never seen him speak with such passion and authority. Sitting up the back, in between Bev and my father (who was wearing slacks—an improvement, just), I found myself wishing that this was my first sight of Dodgy. If I'd met him for the first time tonight, I never would have suspected he was a cad.

The theatre was imbued with the air of film nerddom. I noted a few of the Video Nasties clientele, and Marco, who was up at the front. Next to him was a cool-looking girl I didn't recognise. She had a sixties bob and a cute smile. She was taking notes. She looked like a real film girl, like I was going to be. Tony was there too. He beamed when he saw me and dragged me over to meet the department head.

"This is the girl I was telling you about."

I told the head I was one year away from applying, and that as well as exploring fractured narratives, I was interested in haiku and silent films—how you could tell a story without ever opening your mouth. Word pictures, like my father called it.

Tony said, "She's got the eye. You should see her short. It's like Larry Clark without the perve factor."

My parents pinged with pride.

My *parents*!

And speaking of eyes, I managed to catch Dodgy's just before he sat down for the screening. He smiled and then ducked his head.

"Is that the prick?" my father stage-whispered.

"Shhh!" I passed him a complimentary glass of red wine, and we found our seats. Then someone cut the lights and Warner Brothers bugled us in to *Rebel Without a Cause*.

. . .

I had seen the film before. James Dean's breakthrough role—the birth of the teenager, blah, blah, blah—but Dodgy's speech made me see it in a whole new light. During the shoot, the director, Nicholas Ray, was king of the kids. The young cast would gather at his Chateau Marmont suite on Sunday afternoons to vie for his attention.

According to Hollywood lore, Nicholas Ray seduced Natalie Wood, who then started an affair with Dennis Hopper. There were rumours about Ray and James Dean—both rumoured switch-hitters. The sexually confused Sal Mineo was also crushing on Dean.

For all the rumpy-pumpy, the prevailing mood is loneliness. Ray said, "Look to the father," and they all did. So what looks like a cautionary tale about delinquent youth is really about Jim, Judy, and Plato on a psychological quest to find their father figure in order to find themselves.

Dodgy also said the film was cursed: James Dean died in that horrific smash, Sal Mineo was stabbed to death, and Natalie Wood drowned off the coast of Barbados. Nicholas Ray lived hard, had brain cancer, lost an eye in the cutting room, and died aged sixty-nine.

As I watched the movie, all this information roiled around my head and steeped itself in the story. I was enthralled. I felt like I was seeing the film at the perfect time and that its message rang true for me too. There would be no such tragic end for me. I had a father to look to—even if his presence was only temporary. It was like what we talked about at the reserve. He may have been fleeting, but he'd made his mark.

· · ·

Afterward, Marco and the cool girl came up.

"Awesome Welles! What say you?"

"I liked it," I said. "Dodgy's speech was good."

"He cribbed it," Marco said. "Just kidding. Hey, this is my cousin Amber. She's just moved here."

"Hi." I shook her hand. She had a firm femmo grip.

"Hi—Marco says you're the resident filmmaker."

"I am," I said.

"Well, if you are doing anything filmy, I'm interested."

"Oh, okay, well drop by Video Nasties. I work there too."

She smiled. "I'll do that."

Then Dodgy came up, and we returned to our pre-pash film-noir dialogue form. I said, "Nice speech."

"You think?"

"I know."

"They showed the film in the wrong ratio."

"I didn't notice."

"Who are you with?"

"Bev," I said. "And my dad."

"I didn't know you had a dad."

"There's a lot you don't know about me."

"Hah. Do you want to—"

My father came back and gave Dodgy a smile that was almost violent in its intensity. He grabbed his hand and pumped it. "Rolf Gordon. Proud father. I've seen you before somewhere."

"Okay." Dodgy didn't like where this was going.

"Rolf, this is Dodgy. I work with him." I nodded and then said, "He's in my film." Dodgy cleared his throat. He put his hands in his pockets and jangled his change. He shifted his weight from one leg to the other.

"Ohh, right," Rolf said. "Is he the one who . . . ?"

My mouth turned up, just a little.

Rolf leaned into Dodgy. "You might want to get that checked out." Dodgy went beet red. It was beautiful.

. . .

As the three of us were walking to the car park, I threw a quick backward glance to the foyer window, and I imagined that it was Dodgy silhouetted behind the Japanese screen. He was bending over to tell someone something important. He was the world I could see, but couldn't access. But that was okay.

# *Two or Three Things I Know About My Father*

- His childhood ambition was to be a priest.
- He won an award in grade five for excellent penmanship.
- He was often late for school because if he happened upon a dead animal on the way (be it bird, cat, possum, or roo), he felt compelled to bury it.
- He lost his virginity to an older neighbour after helping her move her piano.
- The first time he asked my mother out she asked him, "Why?" When he couldn't answer on the spot, she sent him away. "Come back when you know." He came back five minutes later saying, "Because I keep dreaming about you."
- He was inspired to write haikus after reading this one by Basho:

*No blossoms and no moon,*
*And he is drinking sake*
*All alone!*

- His favourite book is *In Watermelon Sugar* by Richard Brautigan.
- His favourite album is *Wee Tam and the Big Huge* by the Incredible String Band.
- He can play the banjo.
- He never studied Freud.
- He sometimes gets shingles.
- He's not big on good-byes.

My father left in the wee hours of December 30. I woke up to the sound of blackbirds spooning and dipping in the gutter and instantly knew something had changed. There was an envelope under my door, and inside it was a return ticket on the Spirit of Tasmania. Valid for twelve months. I went back to bed and read *Hunter-Gatherer* from cover to cover. But I didn't cry. Even after all that bad poetry, my eyes stayed dog-bone dry.

# THE EXPLODING PLASTIC INEVITABLE

# *Siberia*

Was it just me, or did HQ seem smaller, darker, damper?

Mira had her compact out and was drawing blue rings around her eyes. Lo was sitting in one of the stalls, smoking as per usual. I had her Jesus T-shirt with me in a plastic bag. The handle was cutting into my wrist.

"It's pissing down," I said, by way of a greeting. "Dark too. It's like winter."

"Dark for dark business," Mira cracked.

The fluorescent strip-light flashed and buzzed above our heads. It was all very noir. I heard the fizz of Lo dropping her fag end in the toilet water. She flushed and sauntered out. Her face was drained of colour; she looked like the underside of a Polaroid.

She handed my dress over. "Thanks for the memories."

"Wow," I said. "You look like shit."

Lo shrugged. "These are testing times."

"Care to elaborate?"

Lo dug in her back pocket and came up with a brightly coloured pamphlet.

"What's this?" I asked. "More art terrorism?"

"Ha-ha." Lo proceeded to read aloud: "Christian Summer Fun Camp. Wholesome fun and a range of challenges for young adults 13–18 . . . white-water rafting, indoor rock-climbing . . ." Lo hesitated and then said, "So as you can see, my parents are trying to take an interest." She sighed. "Once again they are distracted by the loaves and the fishes and the little falling frogs."

"Oh, dear." I started to laugh.

"I know," Lo said dryly.

"But don't they know that Jesus doesn't want you for a sunbeam?"

Lo's lips met in a grim smile. "Yeah, well, they'll work it out."

"How are you going to get out of it?" I asked.

Lo raised her eyebrows at Mira, Mira beamed back.

"After tomorrow night, I'm a ghost," Lo said.

"She's gonna join the Cave Clan." Mira was smiling so hard she looked like a pillhead.

"What?"

"The evil's up here, not down there," Mira-the-Moonie advised me.

"Right." I looked to Lo for some kind of an explanation.

She shook her head. *Don't go there*. Then she lit up again.

"So have you got the film?"

"Yeah," I said. "I wanted to see you both too. I wanted to make sure I wasn't wrong about things."

"What things?" Lo asked. She had a weird, twisted smile on her face. She wanted me to say it. That our friendship was over. Well, I was okay with that.

"I wanted a full stop," I asserted. "Clean and nice."

There was an arc of silence, save for the rain drip-drip-dripping on one of the stainless-steel toilet seats.

Eventually Mira gasped. "Are we in Siberia?"

"I think we're in Siberia," Lo affirmed with a tight smile.

I think I had an image then—I was thinking filmic-ly—two explorers in Nanookian attire were standing on separate ice floes that were drifting slowly, inexorably away from each other. I felt a little artic ache inside.

I took the tapes out of my bag and gave one to Lo and one to Mira.

"Thank fuck," Mira said. She turned to Lo. "I told you she'd come through." But Lo looked at me suspiciously. "What is this—it's not *The F-Word*?"

I shook my head. "*This* is my first film."

Mira was full of questions. "So what is it? When did you do it? Am I even in it?"

I waved my hand. "You wanted a film, I gave you a film. It's got a beginning, a middle, and an end. All you need."

Lo drummed her fingers on the videotape. She stared at me with her small, funny smile.

"Call it a send-off," I said to clarify.

Lo dropped her cigarette butt and let it lie on the cement, smoking to the bitter end. "Okay, then." She linked arms with Mira. "Let's go. Lots to do."

She walked out. Mira followed with a little girl wave. "Ug-ug."

From the doorway I watched them leave. Lo surprised me by turning with what looked like a genuine smile and a salute. "You'd better come tomorrow night," she yelled. "Bring your camera!"

I stayed in the block listening to the rain, smoking and staring at the graffiti. Aside from a Warhol "IT'S A HAPPENING NYE" sticker on the mirror, there was nothing new there. It made me realise that HQ was ours and no one else's. At the start of the year, when we were fresh from Satan Summer and still basking in our high-priestess glow, Mira had drawn practise pentagrams around the air vents. It took her several goes to work out that the pentagram had five points. Dolt! Looking at all our markings gave me pause. What was going to happen next year? There wasn't much point having a headquarters if I was the only person who knew about it. And then I knew that I would never return there—and neither would Lo or Mira.

This was almost too much to think about. Outside the rain kept coming. I shivered. HQ was now a cold tundra.

I felt in my bag for a pen. On the back of the toilet door just under Lo's original flyer I scratched the words "Gem-Lo-Mira RIP." And then I shut my eyes to the rain and started my own run across the swampy oval.

# Pockets of Cool

New Year's Eve at the reserve—the time when our suburb hearkens back to olde worlde days and tries to pretend it's a village once again. According to Bev, the Ferris
Wheel had failed to make the cut, but we could expect
"rockin' sounds" from the brother school grunge band
with the Vince Vaughn look-alike lead singer—goody!

We left the house at sevenish, and the sky was over-
cast. A bad omen, I thought. But the threat of the wet
couldn't deter Bev and Sharon. They had the memory
wall to look forward, and fifteen years of Community
Centre hijinks to drink to. What with that and the return
of Rolf Gordon, I was surprised they hadn't OD'd on nos-
talgia.

Bev was wearing her strapless number again, her hairy
armpits offset by the hibiscus in her hair. Sharon, on
standby as designated driver, had inadvertently gone

eighties butch—court shoes and a dinner suit. Shoulder pads! For my part, I was wearing my brown boho dress with a white frayed fisherman's sweater. I wore my hair down with the fringe swept across my right eye. I had commandeered Rolf's happy-sack, and I was using it as a camera bag. I had the battery charged, lenses polished, and spare tape primed.

I sat in the back of Betsy picking my teeth while Bev checked the oil and water. Sharon twisted in her seatbelt and showed me her teeth. "Another year already."

I said, "It definitely feels like the end of something."

"You should look at it as a new beginning."

"Said the school psychologist."

"Cheeky." Sharon twisted back. "They're expecting big numbers tonight." She started fixing up her foundation-neck in the side mirror.

Bev got in the car and put her seatbelt on, the junky bracelets on her arm jangling. She gave a little piggy squeal and started the engine. "I feel all busy inside! I'm looking forward to the fireworks. It doesn't feel like New Year's without fireworks."

"I heard they're going to be spectacular."

Bev tutted at the sarcastic edge in my voice and turned the radio as she lurched onto the road. The Four Tops did "The Same Old Song," and Bev and Sharon sang along like old women in some cheesy menopausal Hollywood movie, which I guess made me Winona Ryder.

"Hey, Bev," I yelled above the relentlessly jolly guitar break.

"Yessss?"

"Are you going to sneak me some wine tonight?"

"Yessss!"

The Godmother turned with a variation of her Look of Grave Concern.

"Just make sure you have a glass of water in between each drink."

. . .

The Community Centre boasted capacity crowds. Manky teens cruised the trestle tables, scarfing corn chips and vol-au-vents. Malingering olds in dinner dress quaffed the local cheap and nasty wine and tried to locate their younger selves on the memory wall.

As I surveyed the board, my eye was drawn to a photograph of my activist mother, circa 1995. It was taken at the "Wimmins" Market. She was standing behind her stall, all ruddy and positive, the very image of a woman promoting recyclable sanitary pads. I remembered her slogan: "Relinquish your menstrual fears!" I told her they wouldn't catch on.

I sneaked some wine and checked the clock: 7:45 p.m. The room was filling out, and I was starting to feel excited. Was there still going to be a Happening? What form would it take? I was up for audience participation. Strangers were smiling at me. I realised it was because I was smiling at them. I looked for Mira or Lo, or even Alita Bean or Lau Warren, but they were nowhere. I took the video camera out and prepped for shooting.

Half an hour later I was standing in front of the stage
filming the brother school band as they mutilated a
Madonna song when someone tapped my shoulder. I lowered the camera. It was Marco's cousin Amber. She was
wearing a T-shirt with a picture of Tattoo, the midget
from *Fantasy Island*, on it. Above his face were the
words: "Say Hello to my Little Friend."

She nodded to the band. "Jesus, they're appalling."

"How can you say that?" I asked her. "They're the
best the outer east has to offer. Look—they even have
groupies!" Bliss Dartford and Ponyface were sitting on
the speakers. Pony's skirt billowed with the vibrations.

"Tragic." Amber smiled.

Then I saw she had a Warhol "IT'S A HAPPENING
NYE" sticker slapped on her bicep like a sailor's tattoo.

"Where did you get that?" I asked.

"There's a stack of them on the table."

In the silver tray where the napkins should have been
sat a fat wad of stickers, and they were fast disappearing.
I looked around the room. It seemed like anyone under
the age of eighteen had a sticker somewhere on their person. Then I noticed Bev behind the bar—she had Andy
Warhol on each bicep. My cool mum!

Bliss Dartford's father rushed past, browbeating one of
his minions.

"Who's that?" Amber asked.

"Boss Dartford. He's on pyrotechnics."

Amber nodded. "What are we looking at?"

"Well, if it's anything like last year: crackers, catherine

wheels, roman candles, glitter palms, wings, and water-falls."

"Impressive." She nodded to the camera.

"Are you going to film it?"

"That's the idea."

"You could always use the footage for sex scenes." Amber's smile had a good warp to it.

"Boom-boom." I rattled my wrist and we both laughed.

"I like your T-shirt," I told her. "Poor Tattoo. I read his suicide note on the Internet. He said from the age of six he knew he had no place in the world."

"That's so sad. I didn't even know he was dead. She paused and confessed, "I feel kind of awful about it now. I wouldn't want him to think I was laughing at him."

"No." I smiled. "It's a tribute."

Amber and I chatted about her move. She'd come from the inner city—lattes and performance poets—to the outer burbs—land of misspelt cappuccinos and garden centres.

"I'm like *The Girl Who Fell to Earth*," she said.

"Trust me," I assured her. "It's not that bad. There are pockets of cool."

"Oh no, I didn't mean it like that," Amber said quickly. "I'm not a snob, it's just going to be weird, that's all."

Our conversation was fluid, like we'd known each other for ages. And the freaky-best news was that she was going to be at my school, in my year.

She said, "I hate being the new kid."

"I can tell you everything you need to know."

Then the power went out. The Happening was a'happening. I picked up the camera and whispered to Amber, "Action!"

A robotic voice instructed us: "Please remain where you are. Do not attempt to escape."

"What the fuck?" Amber said.

The voice cut off, and a series of lights flashed around the room, illuminating different faces. The crowd were starting to shuffle and arc up until a loud squall silenced them.

I felt Amber squeezing my arm.

"Are you getting this?" she asked.

"Yeah—I don't know how it's going to come out, though." Suddenly a huge screen flashed on. The brother school grunge band moved to the side. A film. It took me several seconds to realise that it was my film.

"That's mine!" I squeaked to Amber.

"Cool!" she whispered back.

I heard the bleatings of the crowd die down, and then I felt an acute anxiety. What if people laughed? What if they hated it? But then I was pulled in. Watching an audience watch my film gave me an emotional overload. I think I was vibrating. The screen illuminated the audience and I panned around to get some reactions. People were staring, rapt, eyes bugging, jaws to the floor. They were nudging each other, recognising faces, behaviours; faces broke into smiles or went botoxed with shock.

My film started with Dodgy and Mira in the gazebo.

And then it went back to the party. I had stacked certain images on top of each other in an attempt to show order in the disorder: There was Cola putting the head of a brass flamingo into his mouth and spouting rap speak. There were Bliss and Pony, posing for the camera, drunk and gibbering, like, like, like. There was Marco pashing Alita Bean. He was eyeing the camera while she had her eyes screwed shut and was dreaming of romance.

Upon seeing her cousin, Amber gasped. And then I heard a yelp, and a voice whining, "Awesome!" Marco was in the audience. I wondered if Dodgy was too. I panned around again. I wished I could see Bev, but she was back behind the bar. I wondered if she'd guessed that this was my handiwork. New scenes unfurled: Mira's stripping—she was luminous. I could hear exclamations of shock from the older faction of the audience. Then there was the snippet of me, Lo, and Mira out of our heads. Funny. It felt like it was filmed years ago. The final shot was an older guy no one knew, going, "All the girls here are sluts and bitches, sluts and bitches!" Then the screen went black. And the lights came back on.

· · ·

The band started up again. They played so loud you couldn't really call it music. It was more like calamity. And now some figures leaped onto the stage. They wore silver tights with silver leotards and animal masks over their faces, but I discerned the Abbott and Costello-ness that was Lau Warren and Alita Bean. This was high interpretative dance. Now they were flailing, now they were marching on the spot, now they were doing the robot. This couldn't have been Lo's idea. It was unendurable. Two more silver figures joined them—Mira, bounding energetically, breasts boinging tribal-style, and J-Roam, keeping it real with his hip-hop manoeuvres, slouch-dancing like he was shifting a wide load in his shorts.

I turned the camera back onto the crowd. They seemed to have settled into the spectacle; all except Boss Dartford. He was striding up toward the stage; his face was set to explode. I kept the camera trained on him. He leaped onto the stage and made for the plasma screen. But the band members moved in front of him to create a fort. Amber and I moved back against the wall and filmed the chaos, open-mouthed. Amber nudged me. "Look!"

Pony was dancing on the amplifier. She saw me filming and "rocked out" with the devil's salute until a loud pop came from the amplifier. She leaped off as the smoke rose up. The band went crazy. The drummer was annihilating his cymbals. The guitarist was scratching his hands up and down his fret board, the bass player was plucking so intensely, it looked like he would topple over, and the Vince Vaughn look-alike lead singer launched a spit-storm, screeching random, unintelligible words into his microphone.

The silver people danced behind the stage and then came forward bearing a stretcher high above their heads. This was Lo. It had to be. But as she was completely wrapped in silver foil—much like a giant spliff—there was no way we could ever know for sure. They brought her through the crowd. As they passed me I heard Lo's voice, "You can always go further."

The crowd did a mass bum part and the dancers carried Lo up the crack, out the door, into the night, down to the river. I hoped there was a silver canoe at the end of it. To take her where she wanted to be, wherever that was.

. . .

The crowd stood in weird formations. Most were facing the stage even though the brother school band had started to pack. A blank belt of silence hung in the air.

Amber said to me, "Do you want to do some vox pops?"

"What are they?"

"You know, random questions, man on the street. You hold the camera, I'll ask the questions."

I grinned at her. "Okay."

Amber grabbed the arm of the first person she saw. It was a winded-looking little old lady. "Excuse me, ma'am, what did you think of the Happening?"

# *Countdown*

10. Amber and I refilled our glasses. We drank greedy gulps.
9. I found my mother, tearing up by the memory wall.
8. She said, "This year is going to be the best year ever."
7. I charged my camera and pressed record.
6. All around me people were folding into each other.
5. Sharon was suffocating Barry "Boobs" Polson.
4. Pony was sucking face with Vince Vaughn.
3. Bliss Dartford was swapping spit with Mark Petrakis.
2. The count was almost down and . . .
1. I didn't even think of looking for someone to kiss.

· · ·

Bev put her hand over the lens and laughed. "Put that thing away!" I grabbed her by her Andy Warhols and hugged her hard. Then I saw Dodgy and Marco leaning on one of the benches. I nudged Amber, and we made our way over to them. Marco had Alita Bean's mask on. He said, "Hey did you hear? Wal's not selling the shop."

"God," I said, "I forgot all about that."

"We made him an offer he couldn't refuse." That was Dodgy, suddenly standing next to me, wearing his old "pachuco" pants and an earnest smile. "Some things should be preserved," he said.

We heard the pop of the first firework and I turned the camera to the sky. The cracker went up maybe ten feet and rocketed back down to earth, leaving a tail of grey fizz. And then all I could hear was anticipation—all the people straining to see the fireworks that never came. How funny. How unspectacular. They were duds. Sabotaged. They tried for ten full minutes. Somewhere Lo was laughing. She'd brought the year in with a whimper and not a bang. Boss Dartford was trying to make a quick getaway, weaving and ducking through boos and raspberries and unidentified flying objects. It was beautiful.

. . .

Amber and I sat in the grass and watched the disappointed masses shuffle back to the Community Centre.

"Talk about anticlimactic," I said.

Amber was pensive. "Imagine if this was the last New Year's we saw."

"It could be," I told her. "World War Three is still up for grabs."

"Shit. And I'm still a virgin." She looked at me. "Uh-oh. Now I've done it. You owe me a secret."

I smiled under the bright stars. There would be plenty of time for that.

# Acknowledgements

Big thanks to the following people for their enthusiasm, input, and support: Melita Granger, Anna McFarlane, Melanie Cecka, Lizzie Spratt, Fran Bryson, Liz Kemp, Jill Grinberg, Arabella Stein, Linda Jaivin, Liz Packett, my friends and family. An early draft of *Notes* was selected for the ASA Emerging Writers Mentorship program.

*The Lipstick Jungle* by Laura Jacobs (*Vanity Fair*, 2004) brought the "three girls" genre home for me. David Thomson's *The Whole Equation—A History of Hollywood* (Knopf, 2004) made me think about why movies matter. Gavin Lambert RIP.